POINT
COUNTERPOINT

Bankruptcy Law

POINT
COUNTERPOINT

Affirmative Action

Amateur Athletics

American Military Policy

Animal Rights

Bankruptcy Law

Blogging

Capital Punishment, Second Edition

Disaster Relief

DNA Evidence

Educational Standards

Election Reform

The FCC and Regulating Indecency

Fetal Rights

Food Safety

Freedom of Speech

Gay Rights

Gun Control

Immigrants' Rights After 9/11

Immigration Policy

Legalizing Marijuana

Mandatory Military Service

Media Bias

Mental Health Reform

Miranda Rights

Open Government

Physician-Assisted Suicide

Policing the Internet

Prescription and Non-prescription Drugs

Prisoners' Rights

Private Property Rights

Protecting Ideas

Religion in Public Schools

The Right to Die

The Right to Privacy

Search and Seizure

Smoking Bans, Second Edition

Stem Cell Research and Cloning

Tort Reform

Trial of Juveniles as Adults

The War on Terror, Second Edition

Welfare Reform

Women in the Military

POINT

COUNTERPOINT

Bankruptcy Law

Sandra Coaxum Allen, J.D., C.P.A.

Series Consulting Editor
Alan Marzilli, M.A., J.D.

CHELSEA HOUSE
PUBLISHERS
An imprint of Infobase Publishing

Bankruptcy Law

Chelsea House
An imprint of Infobase Publishing
132 West 31st Street
New York NY 10001

Library of Congress Cataloging-in-Publication Data

Allen, Sandra Coaxum.
Bankruptcy law / Sandra Coaxum Allen ; series consulting editor, Alan Marzilli.
p. cm. — (Point/counterpoint)
Includes bibliographical references and index.
ISBN 978-0-7910-9713-7 (hardcover)
1. Bankruptcy—United States. 2. Debtor and creditor—United States. I. Title.
KF1524.A85 2008
346.7307'8—dc22 2008027121

Chelsea House books are available at special discounts when purchased in bulk quantities for businesses, associations, institutions, or sales promotions. Please call our Special Sales Department in New York at (212) 967-8800 or (800) 322-8755.

You can find Chelsea House on the World Wide Web at http://www.chelseahouse.com

Series design by Erik Lindstrom
Cover design by Keith Trego and Jooyoung An

Printed in the United States of America

Bang NMSG 10 9 8 7 6 5 4 3 2 1

This book is printed on acid-free paper.

POINT
COUNTERPOINT

FOREWORD

Alan Marzilli, M.A., J.D.
Alabama

The POINT/COUNTERPOINT series offers the reader a greater understanding of some of the most controversial issues in contemporary American society—issues such as capital punishment, immigration, gay rights, and gun control. We have looked for the most contemporary issues and have included topics—such as the controversies surrounding "blogging"—that we could not have imagined when the series began.

In each volume, the author has selected an issue of particular importance and set out some of the key arguments on both sides of the issue. Why study both sides of the debate? Maybe you have yet to make up your mind on an issue, and the arguments presented in the book will help you to form an opinion. More likely, however, you will already have an opinion on many of the issues covered by the series. There is always the chance that you will change your opinion after reading the arguments for the other side. But even if you are firmly committed to an issue—for example, school prayer or animal rights—reading both sides of the argument will help you to become a more effective advocate for your cause. By gaining an understanding of opposing arguments, you can develop answers to those arguments.

Perhaps more importantly, listening to the other side sometimes helps you see your opponent's arguments in a more human way. For example, Sister Helen Prejean, one of the nation's most visible opponents of capital punishment, has been deeply affected by her interactions with the families of murder victims. By seeing the families' grief and pain, she understands much better why people support the death penalty, and she is able to carry out her advocacy with a greater sensitivity to the needs and beliefs of death penalty supporters.

The books in the series include numerous features that help the reader to gain a greater understanding of the issues. Real-life examples illustrate the human side of the issues. Each chapter also includes excerpts from relevant laws, court cases, and other material, which provide a better foundation for understanding the arguments. The volumes contain citations to relevant sources of law and information, and an appendix guides the reader through the basics of legal research, both on the Internet and in the library. Today, through free Web sites, it is easy to access legal documents, and these books might give you ideas for your own research.

Studying the issues covered by the Point-Counterpoint series is more than an academic activity. The issues described in the book affect all of us as citizens. They are the issues that today's leaders debate and tomorrow's leaders will decide. While all of the issues covered in the Point-Counterpoint series are controversial today, and will remain so for the foreseeable future, it is entirely possible that the reader might one day play a central role in resolving the debate. Today it might seem that some debates—such as capital punishment and abortion—will never be resolved.

However, our nation's history is full of debates that seemed as though they never would be resolved, and many of the issues are now well settled—at least on the surface. In the nineteenth century, abolitionists met with widespread resistance to their efforts to end slavery. Ultimately, the controversy threatened the union, leading to the Civil War between the northern and southern states. Today, while a public debate over the merits of slavery would be unthinkable, racism persists in many aspects of society.

Similarly, today nobody questions women's right to vote. Yet at the beginning of the twentieth century, suffragists fought public battles for women's voting rights, and it was not until the passage of the Nineteenth Amendment in 1920 that the legal right of women to vote was established nationwide.

What makes an issue controversial? Often, controversies arise when most people agree that there is a problem, but people disagree about the best way to solve the problem. There is little argument that poverty is a major problem in the United States, especially in inner cities and rural areas. Yet, people disagree vehemently about the best way to address the problem. To some, the answer is social programs, such as welfare, food stamps, and public housing. However, many argue that such subsidies encourage dependence on government benefits while unfairly penalizing those who work and pay taxes, and that the real solution is to require people to support themselves.

American society is in a constant state of change, and sometimes modern practices clash with what many consider to be "traditional values," which are often rooted in conservative political views or religious beliefs. Many blame high crime rates, and problems such as poverty, illiteracy, and drug use on the breakdown of the traditional family structure of a married mother and father raising their children. Since the "sexual revolution" of the 1960s and 1970s, sparked in part by the widespread availability of the birth control pill, marriage rates have declined, and the number of children born outside of marriage has increased. The sexual revolution led to controversies over birth control, sex education, and other issues, most prominently abortion. Similarly, the gay rights movement has been challenged as a threat to traditional values. While many gay men and lesbians want to have the same right to marry and raise families as heterosexuals, many politicians and others have challenged gay marriage and adoption as a threat to American society.

Sometimes, new technology raises issues that we have never faced before, and society disagrees about the best solution. Are people free to swap music online, or does this violate the copyright laws that protect songwriters and musicians' ownership of the music that they create? Should scientists use "genetic engineering" to create new crops that are resistant to disease and pests and produce more food, or is it too risky to use a laboratory to create plants that nature never intended? Modern medicine has continued to increase the average lifespan—which is now 77 years, up from under 50 years at the beginning of the twentieth century—but many people are now choosing to die in comfort rather than living with painful ailments in their later years. For doctors, this presents an ethical dilemma: should they allow their patients to die? Should they assist patients in ending their own lives painlessly?

Perhaps the most controversial issues are those that implicate a Constitutional right. The Bill of Rights—the first 10 Amendments to the U.S. Constitution—spell out some of the most fundamental rights that distinguish our democracy from other nations with fewer freedoms. However, the sparsely-worded document is open to interpretation, with each side saying that the Constitution is on their side. The Bill of Rights was meant to protect individual liberties; however, the needs of some individuals clash with society's needs. Thus, the Constitution often serves as a battleground between individuals and government officials seeking to protect society in some way. The First Amendment's guarantee of "freedom of speech" leads to some very difficult questions. Some forms of expression—such as burning an American flag—lead to public outrage, but are protected by the First Amendment. Other types of expression that most people find objectionable—such as child pornography—are not protected by the Constitution. The question is not only where to draw the line, but whether drawing lines around constitutional rights threatens our liberty.

The Bill of Rights raises many other questions about individual rights and societal "good." Is a prayer before a high school football game an "establishment of religion" prohibited by the First Amendment? Does the Second Amendment's promise of "the right to bear arms" include concealed handguns? Does stopping and frisking someone standing on a known drug corner constitute "unreasonable search and seizure" in violation of the Fourth Amendment? Although the U.S. Supreme Court has the ultimate authority in interpreting the U.S. Constitution, their answers do not always satisfy the public. When a group of nine people—sometimes by a five-to-four vote—makes a decision that affects hundreds of millions of others, public outcry can be expected. For example, the Supreme Court's 1973 ruling in Roe v. Wade that abortion is protected by the Constitution did little to quell the debate over abortion.

Whatever the root of the controversy, the books in the Point-Counterpoint series seek to explain to the reader both the origins of the debate, the current state of the law, and the arguments on either side of the debate. Our hope in creating this series is that readers will be better informed about the issues facing not only our politicians, but all of our nation's citizens, and become more actively involved in resolving these debates, as voters, concerned citizens, journalists, or maybe even elected officials.

Bankruptcy Abuse Prevention and Consumer Protection Act of 2005

> There was a time when a fool and his money were soon parted, but now it happens to everybody.
>
> —Adlai E. Stevenson, U.S. vice president 1893–1897

In December 2007, the *Detroit News* profiled a couple, Sarah and Ed Horton, who had been juggling medical and credit card bills since their 2001 wedding. The couple said they had planned to use their credit cards only for emergencies, but then buying gasoline for their cars and groceries for their family of four turned into "emergencies." Earlier in 2007, they were forced to sell their two cars and move in with Sarah Horton's father. The collection calls from creditors were so overwhelming, they ended up filing for bankruptcy.

If the Hortons had filed for bankruptcy a couple of years earlier, the process probably would have been much easier for them. In 2005, though, the U.S. Congress changed the country's bankruptcy laws and passed the new Bankruptcy Abuse Prevention and Consumer Protection Act (BAPCPA). The Hortons therefore had to follow a more complex procedure when they filed for bankruptcy. Nevertheless, after endless meetings with credit counselors, bankruptcy court trustees, and creditors, their debt was wiped out. The *Detroit News* reported that Sarah Horton felt that filing for bankruptcy had been the right choice for them, "but [she] knows her troubles aren't over. For the next 10 years, the [bankruptcy] will remain on their individual credit reports and can hurt their ability to obtain credit, get a mortgage or rental contract, and even raise red flags with prospective employers."[1] Despite the difficulties and embarrassment of bankruptcy, though, Sarah Horton believed that it gave them "a clean slate, a chance to make a life" for their family.[2]

The Hortons may be better off now, but what about those who extended credit to them in good faith? They relied on the couple's promise to repay. To recover the bad debt, their creditors are likely to pass on the cost to other consumers through increased interest rates. Is it fair for other borrowers to pay higher fees and interest just because the Hortons were unable to meet their obligations? The U.S. Constitution requires Congress to enact bankruptcy laws, so there is no question that the Hortons have the right to seek bankruptcy protection. The challenge that Congress faces is how to balance the rights and needs of creditors against the debtors' need to find relief when unavoidable circumstances prevent them from paying their bills.

Debtors filing for bankruptcy argue that they find themselves in financial crises through no fault of their own—that unforeseen circumstances, such as unexpected unemployment, long-term illness, and other catastrophic events, force them to make choices that lead to financial ruin. Creditors, on the other hand, insist that debtors create financial crises by overusing their credit cards and borrowing more than they can repay, by spending recklessly, and by mismanaging their personal finances.

Perhaps it is true that many families fail to manage their credit card debt properly. Research shows that since 1989, credit card debt in the United States has tripled. It increased more than 30 percent from 2000 to 2005.[3] Because of this continued increase in credit card debt, along with unemployment and rising medical costs, the number of consumer bankruptcies increased from 616,000 in 1989 to more than 1.8 million in 2004.[4] These findings are consistent with the results of a national survey of

New York post-bankruptcy reform study challenges earlier findings.

The Institute for Financial Literacy (IFL), an approved consumer credit counseling organization, analyzed bankruptcy filers after the Bankruptcy Abuse Prevention and Consumer Protection Act (BAPCPA) of 2005 went into effect.

The IFL findings disputed earlier studies of those who file for bankruptcy and the reasons for their financial distress. Previous studies had found that more than half of bankruptcies were due to medical debt. The IFL study found only about 30 percent of bankruptcies due to medical debt and that more than half the clients who participated were overextended on credit, with almost the same percentage reporting filing due to "unexpected expenses."

According to this study, job loss or reduction in wages is by far the most important cause of severe financial problems among middle-class families. These financial problems ultimately lead to bankruptcy. More than 45 percent of the clients who participated in the IFL study had experienced a reduction in their income and more than 32 percent had lost a job.

The IFL plans to continue to study its clients to analyze the causes and issues surrounding bankruptcy. Clients who come to the organization are given the option of participating in the study.

Source: "New York post-bankruptcy reform study challenges earlier findings." *Daily Record* (Rochester, N.Y. May 25, 2006).

1,150 phone interviews with households whose income had fallen between 50 percent and 120 percent of their local median income. The participants must have had credit card debt for three months or longer at the time of the survey.[5] The national survey found that people who have lost their jobs or who have no health insurance are twice as likely to use credit for living expenses. It also found that 1 out of 3 low- to middle-income households uses credit for basics such as food and utilities.[6]

These statistics are staggering. Often, families have had no good choice. If one income earner in the family loses his or her job, or if someone becomes seriously ill, the family may have to turn to credit to cover their basic needs. According to the American Bar Association, "approximately 90 percent of bankruptcies are the result of unemployment, medical bills, or divorce. The remaining 10 percent are due to a variety of factors—including the failure of a business or overuse of credit cards."[7]

If these statistics are accurate, then what recourse do people have when faced with unemployment, major illness, or other crippling circumstances? Indeed, the need for bankruptcy protection is as great today as ever. Consumer advocates are concerned that the new provisions of BAPCPA make it more difficult to file and have a chilling effect on debtors who genuinely need bankruptcy protection. Before 2005, people in financial distress could file for bankruptcy with relative ease and avoid having to pay off their credit cards and other debts. They could complete the required forms without the assistance of an attorney, and file with very little cost. Now, not only do the new provisions increase the cost of filing, but debtors also must hire an attorney. Bankruptcy attorneys have increased their fees since they may now be liable if the information provided by the debtor is not correct. Moreover, debtors are now required to get credit counseling before filing and take a financial management course at the end of the bankruptcy process.

Supporters of the new bankruptcy law say this is exactly as it should be. Families who find themselves in financial crises must bear some of the responsibility for their condition. Opponents of the Act, however, say the new bankruptcy laws go too far. They contend that ultimately debtors who do not file will be worse off: Their illnesses may turn into disabilities because they cannot pay

Financial Stress Survey

A research project was conducted in November of 2005 to assess the effects of credit card debt on adults in the United States. The survey was conducted online with a random sample of 1,517 adults who closely match U.S. population demographics, and who carry credit card debt.

The survey concluded that six in ten of the respondents report carrying credit card debt, and more than two-thirds of them received their first credit card when they were 24 or younger. Just over half of them used their credit cards for groceries and gas. The second highest category, at 46 percent, was clothing and beauty products. Gifts, the third highest category, were purchased with credit cards by 42 percent of the respondents who carried credit card debt.

Respondents constantly used their credit cards even though more than one-third of those with credit card debt fear that they will never get out of debt. Despite these fears, respondents continue to spend.

A similar survey was conducted in October of 2006 to assess holiday shopping plans and finances. Approximately 55 percent of respondents said that finances are their main source of stress during the holiday season, yet almost 52 percent use their credit cards for at least some of the holiday shopping. They also planned to spend about the same on the holidays as they did in the previous year.

This pattern of continued spending affects more than credit card use and extends beyond the holiday season. More than 60 percent of respondents felt that their current savings were inadequate for emergencies or unexpected job loss. Sixty-seven percent of women felt their savings were inadequate, compared to only 54 percent of the men. Both women and men believed you should have more than six months of living expenses in savings and that their current savings would cover less than three months of household living expenses.

Source: "Research Report: Annual Financial Stress Survey" (November 7, 2005), and "Research Report: Holiday Spending & Financial Stress Survey" (October 30, 2006). Available online at www.familycredit.org/news/publications.cfm.

for medical care. Their families could become homeless because they cannot pay rent. Their children might have to drop out of school to work, leading to lower earnings for them as adults.[8] This is not what Congress wanted to happen.

Who is right? Is the new bankruptcy law effective in curbing abuses while providing protection for those debtors who need it? It may be years before the answer is known.

What Is Bankruptcy?

The American Bar Association defines *bankruptcy* as "a legal process through which people and businesses can seek to obtain fresh financial starts when they cannot pay their debts as agreed."[9] A *debt* is an amount of money that an individual or business owes to another individual or business because of a loan, credit, or some other contractual obligation. The *debtor* is the one who owes money to another. The *creditor* is the one to whom the money is owed. A debtor qualifies for bankruptcy if either his or her monthly expenses exceed income or if liabilities (what the debtor owes) exceed assets (what the debtor has).

The Roots of *Bankruptcy*

The term bankruptcy comes from two Latin words meaning "bench" and "break." Thus, *bankruptcy* literally means "broken bench." Under Roman law, after gathering together and dividing up the assets of a delinquent debtor, the creditors would break the debtor's workbench as a punishment and a warning to other indebted tradesmen. Bankrupt individuals were regarded as thieves who deserved severe punishment. Romans deprived such persons of their civil rights. Many other societies punished bankrupt individuals by requiring them to dress in particular, identifying clothes.

Source: Crown Financial Ministries, "Bankruptcy," http://www.crown.org/pamphlets/pdfs/Bankruptcy.pdf.

Bankruptcy relief starts when the debtor files a *bankruptcy petition* with a bankruptcy court. The bankruptcy petition lists all of the debtor's assets, liabilities, income, and expenses. As soon as the debtor files the petition, creditors must immediately stop their collection efforts. This is called an *automatic stay*, and is usually in effect throughout the bankruptcy process.

Key Legal Terms

automatic stay: An injunction that automatically stops lawsuits, foreclosures, garnishments, and all collection activity against the debtor the moment a bankruptcy petition is filed.

bankruptcy estate: All legal or equitable interests of the debtor in property at the time of the bankruptcy filing. (The estate includes all property in which the debtor has an interest, even if it is owned or held by another person.)

bankruptcy petition: The document filed by the debtor (in a voluntary case) or by creditors (in an involuntary case) that opens the bankruptcy case. (There are official forms for bankruptcy petitions.)

trustee: The representative of the bankruptcy estate who exercises statutory powers, principally for the benefit of the unsecured creditors, under the general supervision of the court and the direct supervision of the U.S. trustee or bankruptcy administrator. The trustee is a private individual or corporation appointed in all Chapter 7, Chapter 12, and Chapter 13 cases and some Chapter 11 cases. The trustee's responsibilities include reviewing the debtor's petition and schedules and bringing actions against creditors or the debtor to recover property of the bankruptcy estate. In Chapter 7, the trustee liquidates property of the estate, and makes distributions to creditors. Trustees in Chapters 12 and 13 have similar duties to a Chapter 7 trustee and the additional responsibilities of overseeing the debtor's plan, receiving payments from debtors, and disbursing plan payments to creditors.

Source: U. S. Courts—Bankruptcy Basics. Available online at www.uscourts.gov/bankruptcycourts/bankruptcybasics/glossary.html.

The BAPCPA identifies the two basic types of bankruptcies for which a person can file. The two types are referred to as *Chapter 7* (liquidation) and *Chapter 13* (rehabilitation) bankruptcy. When a person files for bankruptcy, the court either eliminates at least a portion of that person's existing debts (Chapter 7) or stretches out the monthly payments on those debts with the court's protection and supervision (Chapter 13).

The new law establishes a *means test* that directs debtors to file for either Chapter 7 or Chapter 13, based on their ability to repay creditors. Before bankruptcy reform, debtors were allowed to choose the type of bankruptcy they wanted to use. Most debtors chose to file under Chapter 7, which offered relief so long as there was no evidence of substantial abuse. Filing under Chapter 7 required debtors to repay creditors out of the proceeds from the sale of property the debtor already owned.[10] The debtor's obligation to repay in bankruptcy had very little to do with his or her personal income.

The BAPCPA abolished the debtor's right to choose between the two kinds of bankruptcy. The Act substituted a new means test to determine whether a debtor is allowed to file under Chapter 7, based on the debtor's average monthly *earnings* during the six-month period prior to filing.[11] If the debtor's income exceeds his or her expenses, or if the debtor's average income is higher than the state median income, then he or she must file under Chapter 13. The debtor then enters into a court-ordered arrangement to pay creditors regularly from earned wages, usually over a three- to five-year period.

Another major change under the BAPCPA reform is to require those seeking bankruptcy protection to consult with an "approved nonprofit budget and credit counseling agency" before filing the petition. This pre-petition counseling requirement generated considerable controversy during the first year after the Act's passage.

Legal Foundation

Article I, Section 8, Clause 4 of the U.S. Constitution authorizes Congress to pass "uniform laws on the subject of bankruptcies throughout the United States." Since 1800, Congress has exercised this power through the enactment of five different national bankruptcy acts, which represent the uniform federal law that governs all bankruptcy cases. The most recent national bankruptcy act is the Bankruptcy Abuse Prevention and Consumer Protection Act of 2005 (BAPCPA), effective October 17, 2005.[12] President George W. Bush signed the act into law on April 20, 2005. Also known as the Bankruptcy Reform Act, the BAPCPA is the most comprehensive revision to the nation's bankruptcy system in more than a quarter of a century.

What led to this drastic revision in bankruptcy laws? Bankruptcy reform was prompted in part by the significant increase in filings since 1978, by more than 250 percent from 1989 to 2004.[13] By 2004, more Americans were filing for bankruptcy each year than were graduating from college. From 1980 to 2004, credit card debt per household increased from 3.2 percent of the median family income to 12.5 percent.[14] It was also becoming increasingly difficult for creditors to recover payments from debtors seeking bankruptcy protection. Bankruptcy-reform advocates long alleged that consumers abused the law by filing for bankruptcy even when they could afford to repay at least some of their debts. After years of arguing this, the reform advocates succeeded in changing the laws.

The new law makes it harder for an individual to file a Chapter 7 bankruptcy, which extinguishes a person's debts. As a result of this change, it is easier for creditors to be repaid over time. Banks, credit card companies, retailers, and automobile manufacturers are happy about the changes. Critics, however, say the new law places additional burdens on middle-income families, while at the same time keeping open loopholes that benefit the wealthy.

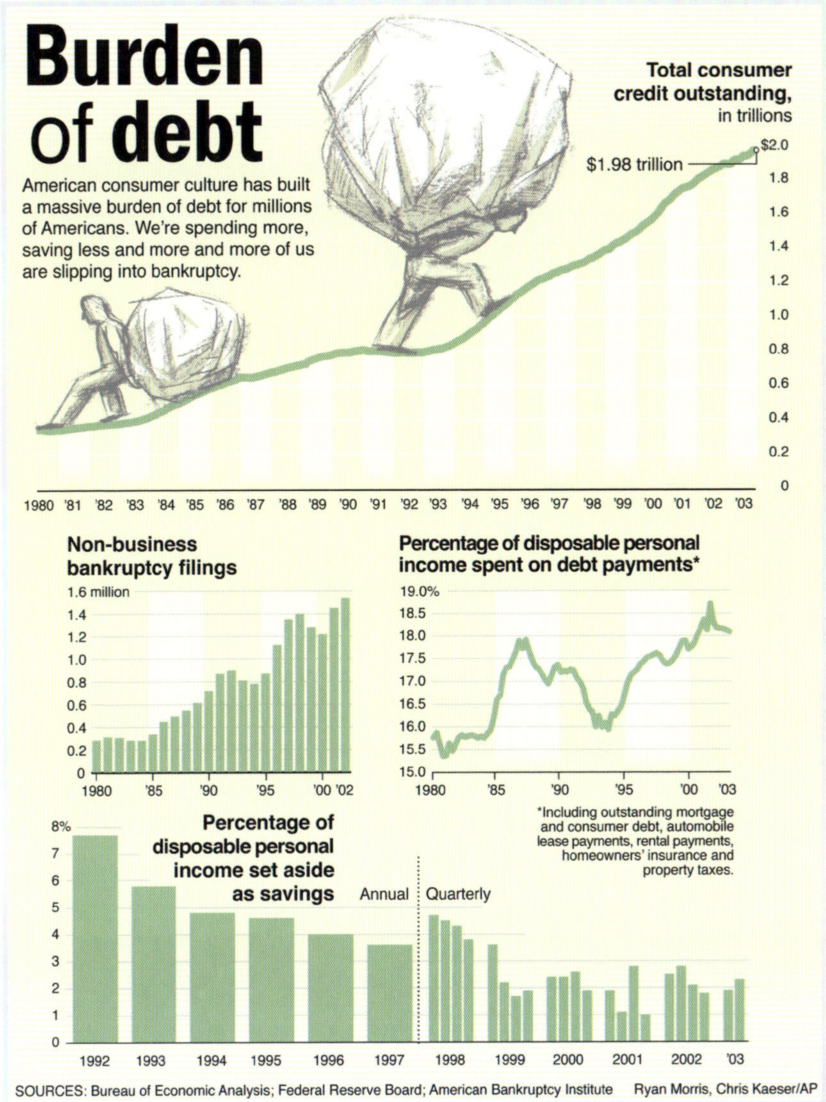

More and more Americans are finding themselves in crises of debt, which may lead to bankruptcy. The graphs above show some of the trends in the finances of Americans.

The body of bankruptcy law includes more than just constitutional and legislative law. Federal judicial districts handle bankruptcy matters, and in almost all of the 94 federal judicial districts, bankruptcy cases are filed in a special bankruptcy court. Thus, federal bankruptcy judges have shaped bankruptcy law through their court decisions as to how the bankruptcy law will be applied in each individual case. Their decisions may range from whether or not a debtor is eligible to file for bankruptcy at all, to whether or not the debtor must pay a particular creditor.

The U.S. Supreme Court has also played an active role in developing bankruptcy laws. It explained the purpose of bankruptcy law in the 1934 decision for *Local Loan Co. v. Hunt*. The Supreme Court said that bankruptcy law "gives to the honest but unfortunate debtor . . . a new opportunity in life and a clear field for future effort, unhampered by the pressure and discouragement of preexisting debt."[15]

Much of the bankruptcy process is administrative and does not include the direct involvement of the bankruptcy judge. This administrative process is generally handled by a "trustee" the bankruptcy judge appoints to oversee the case. The trustee, attorneys, and the bankruptcy judge must all follow the Federal Rules of Bankruptcy Procedure,[16] which are issued by the Administrative Office of the United States Courts. This office, created in 1939, provides a wide range of administrative, legal, financial, management, program, and information technology services to the federal courts.[17]

Chapter 7: Liquidation, or "Straight Bankruptcy"

Chapter 7 bankruptcy is used primarily by debtors who lack the ability to pay their existing debts. A Chapter 7 *liquidation*, also known as *straight bankruptcy*, begins with the filing of a bankruptcy petition in the U.S. Bankruptcy Court. A consumer or a business can file a Chapter 7 bankruptcy, usually to get rid either of unsecured debts or secured debts for property that the debtor no longer wants to keep.

An *unsecured debt* is one where the creditor has no guarantee of repayment. The creditor extends credit based solely on an assessment of the debtor's ability to repay the debt. Credit card debt, medical or legal bills, and utility bills are all examples of unsecured debt. A *secured debt* is one that a creditor is entitled to collect by repossessing and selling the debtor's property if payments are missed. A debt becomes secured if, at the time the loan is made, both the debtor and the creditor agree that if the debtor does not make payments, then the creditor can take ownership of the items purchased (such as a home, vehicle, furniture, or kitichen appliances); or the creditor can take ownership of items that the debtor already owns (such as a stock portfolio or valuable piece of art).

The Chapter 7 filing can be *involuntary*, where the creditors start the process, or *voluntary*, where the debtor starts the process. The vast majority of Chapter 7 filings are voluntary. By filing the petition, the debtor seeks the court's protection in ordering creditors to *stay*, or halt, collection activities. To qualify for this *automatic stay*, the debtor's petition must include information about assets, liabilities, income, and expenses. The debtor must also provide copies of tax returns, photo identification, evidence of recent payments from employers, as well as a certificate to prove that he or she participated in credit counseling within 180 days of filing.

Once the debtor files the petition, the bankruptcy judge assigns a trustee to the case. The bankruptcy trustee is a government official who controls the *bankruptcy estate* for the duration of the case. The bankruptcy estate consists of all the property the debtor owns when he or she files for bankruptcy. The trustee collects the debtor's property, sells the property, and distributes the proceeds of the sale to the creditors. A secured creditor will receive the *collateral*—the secured property itself or the proceeds from the sale of the collateral. After paying the secured debts, the trustee distributes proceeds from the sale of unsecured property among the unsecured creditors. For example, if the sale of all of the unsecured property brings in $5,000, and the total owed to unsecured creditors is $50,000, then each unsecured creditor receives 10 percent of the amount owed to that creditor.

Although the bankruptcy judge makes the final decision, the bankruptcy trustee oversees the process and makes an official recommendation as to whether or not the debts will be discharged. A *discharge* is a court order that is issued at the end of a bankruptcy case. The discharge cancels certain debts that the debtor had when the bankruptcy was filed. Unless one of the creditors objects or some other unforeseen problem arises, the discharge usually occurs four to six months after the filing under Chapter 7.

After the discharge, the debtor has very little, if any, property left. The good news is that the prior debt is eliminated and the debtor has no duty to repay the discharged debts. The slate is wiped clean. Thus, in a Chapter 7 bankruptcy case, the debtor

Types of Bankruptcy

Chapter 7 of the Bankruptcy Code is available to both individual and business debtors. Property is liquidated and then distributed to creditors. Unsecured debts are discharged, thereby giving the debtor a fresh financial start.

Chapter 11 of the Bankruptcy Code is available to both individual and business debtors. It is generally used by a corporation or partnership to keep a business alive, but it can also be used to reorganize an individual's finances. Creditors are paid over time through a court-approved reorganization plan.

Chapter 12 of the Bankruptcy Code is designed to give special debt relief to a family farmer or a family fisherman.

Chapter 13 of the Bankruptcy Code is available for an individual with regular income whose debts do not exceed specified amounts. It allows a debtor to keep property and to pay his or her debt over time, usually three to five years.

Source: Adapted from U. S. Courts—Bankruptcy Basics. Available online at www.uscourts.gov/bankruptcycourts/bankruptcybasics/glossary.html.

gets a fresh start and is free of most debts. This is one of the primary purposes of the bankruptcy system.

Chapter 13: Rehabilitation, or "Wage Earner Bankruptcy"

Individuals with regular income who would like to pay all or part of their debts in installments over time file for Chapter 13 bankruptcy, referred to as *wage earner bankruptcy*. Chapter 13 does not apply to businesses. It is generally used when a debtor has secured debts and the property is threatened with foreclosure (the legal process in which the lender sells the property, such as a home, and keeps the proceeds to pay off the debt) or repossession (the lender takes the property back from the debtor). Unlike under Chapter 7, a Chapter 13 filer can keep the secured property even if he or she is behind on the payments when the Chapter 13 bankruptcy petition is filed. The debtor must repay some or all of the debt over the course of the repayment plan.

In its *Guide to Credit and Bankruptcy*, the American Bar Association explains:

> Chapter 13 is available to almost everyone who has a regular income. The only other requirement is that you have less than $307,675 in unsecured debts (such as credit card debts) and less than $922,975 in secured debts (such as home mortgages and car loans). . . . Anyone with greater debts usually must declare bankruptcy under chapters 7 or 11 of the Bankruptcy Code.[18]

A Chapter 13 bankruptcy, like a straight bankruptcy under Chapter 7, begins with the filing of a bankruptcy petition and the assignment of a trustee. Only the debtor may file a Chapter 13 petition. There are no involuntary Chapter 13 cases, unlike in Chapter 7, where creditors can force debtors into bankruptcy. In a Chapter 13 case, the repayment plan generally lasts three to five years, continuing until the debtor has made all of the payments required by the plan. Throughout the course of the repayment plan, creditors are forbidden from contacting the debtor about the debts—no phone calls, no letters. The debtor receives a bankruptcy discharge after completing the repayment plan.[19]

The Consumer Credit Counseling Controversy

Another controversial change to bankruptcy law requires debtors to go through consumer credit counseling before they file for bankruptcy. A debtor cannot file for bankruptcy unless he or she has completed this counseling, either one-on-one with an adviser or in a group. The counseling must occur within 180 days before filing the bankruptcy petition. The new law also requires debtors to complete an "instructional course concerning personal financial management" prior to final discharge. The two-hour class is intended to teach good budget management.

A representative from the Coalition for the Implementation of Bankruptcy Reform, made up of major trade associations and consumer credit businesses, testified before Congress regarding financial counseling for debtors:

> During the 9 years of deliberations on the Act, it became all too clear that many consumers file for bankruptcy without ever realizing that it is possible to resolve their financial difficulties in more constructive ways. The Act seeks to address this issue by requiring consumers to obtain basic education before filing for bankruptcy.... This is one of the most important consumer benefits included in the Act. It creates an opportunity for consumers to avoid filing for bankruptcy if their financial condition enables them to do so. In order to ensure that this provision is effective, it is imperative that the U.S. Trustee approves only counseling agencies of the highest quality.[20]

The new law directs consumer credit counselors to help debtors explore the possibility of repaying debts outside of bankruptcy and to educate the debtor about credit, budgeting, and financial management.

Some credit counseling agencies and credit repair organizations, however, are scam operations that harm the debtor, so the Federal Trade Commission (FTC) regulates and monitors the activities of these organizations. Established by the Federal Trade Commission Act in 1914 during the presidency of Woodrow Wilson, the FTC protects consumers against unfair or deceptive business practices through its Bureau of Consumer Protection; it also prevents business practices that may impair competition among businesses through its Bureau of Competition.

In *Federal Trade Commission v. AmeriDebt, Inc. et al.*, the FTC sued counseling agencies AmeriDebt and DebtWorks, as well as the companies' founder, Andris Pukke, for misrepresentations and fraudulent practices. The FTC charged that AmeriDebt deceived consumers with claims that it was a nonprofit organization and that it provided counseling services to consumers seeking to get out of debt. According to the FTC, instead of operating for charitable purposes as advertised, AmeriDebt funneled profits to affiliated for-profit entities and individuals, including DebtWorks and Pukke. The FTC settled the 2003 complaint in January 2006 for up to $35 million to be paid by AmeriDebt.[21]

Summary

The Bankruptcy Abuse Prevention and Consumer Protection Act of 2005 makes sweeping changes to the bankruptcy system in the United States, affecting the rights of creditors, debtors, and bankruptcy attorneys.

This book will focus on the legal and practical effects that the Act's most controversial changes have on consumers. Do the changes in the law effectively reduce abuse in the bankruptcy system, or has the result been "business as usual"? Do these revisions make it easier for creditors to recover outstanding debts when debtors face financial disasters, or are debtors just as likely to file for bankruptcy as they were before? Does mandatory consumer credit counseling assist the debtor in finding better alternatives to bankruptcy, or is it just another moneymaking scheme for the financial industry? What happens when a consumer is hit with unemployment and is thus unable to pay off debts? Even as creditors bombard the debtor with phone calls and letters demanding immediate payment, the debtor may have no source of income and no assets that he or she can convert to cash. What are the options? Is bankruptcy the answer?

Recent Reforms Help Prevent Abuse of Bankruptcy Laws

New bankruptcy laws protect the American family.

The U.S. Constitution requires Congress to enact uniform laws allowing businesses and consumers to cancel and to restructure debt obligations.[1] The government, therefore, has an interest in protecting the economic stability of the American family.

Attorney Max Gardner suggests that there is a biblical basis for the government's interest in balancing the obligation to pay debt against the preservation of the family unit. He writes:

> The Bible [in Leviticus 25:39] makes it clear that people are generally expected to pay their debts.... However, this moral and legal obligation to pay just debts must be balanced by . . . the need for compassion.... [T]he Old Testament is replete with examples of compassionate treatment of the poor,

> and with preservation of the family unit. These goals were superior to the material concerns of repayment of debt. . . . The Old Testament model can therefore be legitimately applied to modern day bankruptcy laws. The principle is that, while taken seriously, debt can be canceled to achieve some higher purpose—such as the preservation of the family unit.[2]

The bankruptcy system protects the American family while ensuring that creditors will receive at least a portion of what is owed to them. And yet, over the years, some families have used the bankruptcy system less and less responsibly. Instead of filing for bankruptcy as a last resort, certain consumers use the system as a way of avoiding their responsibilities. There is no "higher purpose." If they repeatedly spend more money than they earn, they can simply file for bankruptcy. The incentive to manage the family budget in a more responsible way has been replaced by the desire to have it all, and now.

The revised bankruptcy system provides incentives for families to better manage their finances. Specifically, bankruptcy provisions:

- Require debtors to get consumer credit counseling to educate them about personal financial management.
- Require debtors to wait several years before filing again, thus forcing them to pay closer attention to personal finances and to avoid future bankruptcies.
- Protect debtors from continued harassment by zealous debt collectors. (Creditors cannot collect from the debtor during the bankruptcy process, nor can they collect discharged debts after the bankruptcy.)
- Provide debtors the opportunity for a fresh financial start.

New provisions reduce the number of repeat filings.

Congress recently reformed the bankruptcy laws to make it harder for individuals to use the system to avoid paying their debts. In the past, some individuals repeatedly filed for bankruptcy with no intention of completing the process: They filed petitions just to create an automatic stay that prevented creditors from seizing their assets or wages. In this way, the bankruptcy petition had the sole purpose of delaying collection or foreclosure activities. By making one filing after another, a person could misuse the system and keep creditors at bay almost indefinitely.

Supporters of bankruptcy reform say that the new provisions have had the desired effects—fewer repeat filings and less abuse of the system. During the first year after the changes, the number of bankruptcy filings decreased by more than 60 percent. This is partly because consumers now must pass a "*means test*" before filing for Chapter 7 bankruptcy. Since people who try to abuse the bankruptcy system do so to avoid their debt completely, they are unwilling to file under Chapter 13, which requires a repayment plan.

Another reason that a debtor is less likely to abuse the new system is that he or she must wait longer before filing for another bankruptcy. That requirement, coupled with the fact that attorneys now must verify their clients' financial information before filing, deters debtors from abusing the system. In addition, some categories of debt that could be discharged under the old law—such as student loans from private lenders—cannot be discharged under the new provisions.

Tougher laws ultimately reduce the cost of debt.

In 2006, about 150 million Americans, including college and high school students, had credit cards. This was 80 percent more people than 15 years ago. Although having access to credit cards might appear to be good for the economy because it boosts consumer spending, that is only part of the story. Credit card spending has a

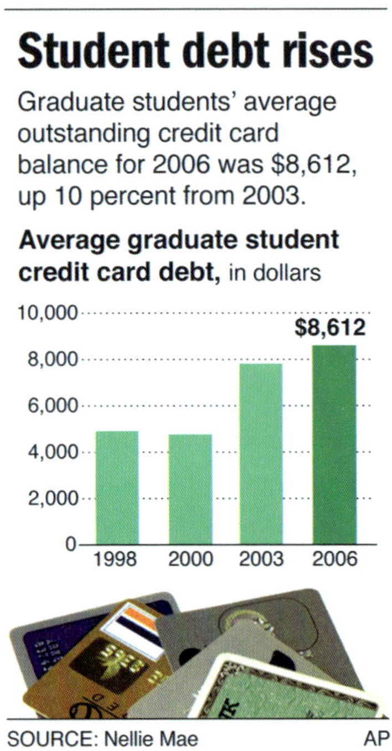

As more people come to rely on credit cards, debt rises. In particular, students of higher education (college and graduate school) have assumed more debt each year.

hidden cost: debt. As the number of credit card holders rose, the dollar amount of credit card debt grew about 350 percent over the last 15 years. In fact, one-third of bankruptcy filers have more than a year's salary of debt from credit cards alone. This amount does not include mortgage debt, student loans, or automobile loans.

The new bankruptcy provisions reduce the societal cost of debt. By requiring debtors to pass a means test, the bankruptcy laws force more debtors to file under Chapter 13, which allows creditors to recover a larger portion of the outstanding debt. If a person who has already been through bankruptcy goes on to accumulate debts again, creditors may charge this person higher interest rates and penalties. This is justified because it allows creditors to offset lost profit from bank discharges.[3] As a result, the creditor need not pass on the cost of riskier debts to consumers who have good credit and who regularly pay down their debts.

Another way in which the new bankruptcy provisions tend to reduce the cost of debt is that now debtors who wish to file for bankruptcy must first receive consumer credit counseling. They also receive additional financial management training before receiving a final discharge. These people will, arguably, do a better job of managing their personal finances and are less likely to neglect credit card payments or other debts. Prior to 2005, bankruptcy filers were no better equipped to manage their finances after bankruptcy than they were before they filed.

Summary

The bankruptcy system is designed to provide the American family unit with some relief when it goes through financial crises. The new 2005 provisions equip families to make better decisions when financial crises arise, and more importantly, to avoid a crisis altogether.

Debtors must now give much more thought to the decision to file for bankruptcy. They can no longer afford to use the bankruptcy process merely as a delay tactic. Certain requirements, such as the means test, act as deterrents to debtors who might otherwise try to abuse the system by repeatedly filing for bankruptcy to avoid or delay legitimate efforts to collect debts. Also, because debtors are now required to go through pre- and post-bankruptcy counseling, they become more financially aware and are less likely to default on credit card bills and other debts in the future. This results in fewer repeat filings, as well as a reduction in the dollar amount of national credit card debt.

COUNTERPOINT

Recent Reforms Delay the Debtor's Fresh Start

The means test causes delay.

If the purpose of bankruptcy is to give the debtor a fresh start, then why has bankruptcy reform made the process so difficult? In the past, consumers could choose the type of bankruptcy under which they would file. They usually preferred to file under Chapter 7 (liquidation) because it gave them a fresh start by offering an immediate discharge from most of their debts.

Now consumers whose average monthly income exceeds their state's median income cannot file under Chapter 7. This test of their financial means, along with other major changes made by the 2005 reform, makes it more difficult for people to file under Chapter 7. If a debtor fails the means test (if his or her income exceeds the state median), he or she can voluntarily change the filing from Chapter 7 to Chapter 13 without having to pay another filing fee. However, a court cannot convert a Chapter 7 to a Chapter 13 unless the debtor consents. If the debtor refuses to consent, then the court will dismiss the case outright. If the case is dismissed, the debtor must file a new petition and start the process over from the beginning.

With the means test, the likelihood is very high that a Chapter 13 case will be converted to a Chapter 7 case. With no increase in income, families are expected to repay their debts over a three- to five-year period under the approved repayment plan. A member of the National Association of Consumer Bankruptcy Attorneys explains the irony of this situation:

> Under the old law, a court would not approve a Chapter 13 plan unless it was clear that the debtor's *actual* income could support a plan over three to five years. Under the new law, the court decides whether to approve a plan based on a figure that does not necessarily reflect your actual income. Instead, the court looks at the debtor's average income over the six-month period prior to filing even though the debtor's current income may be much less. The result of this fiction is that many Chapter 13 plans that appear feasible under the new law will in fact be doomed to failure.[1]

With steady increases in the cost of living and a declining job market, debtors may be unable to make the scheduled payments. If a debtor does not comply with the Chapter 13 repayment plan, the court may dismiss the case or convert it back to a Chapter 7, which the debtor filed in the first place, knowing that he or she could not keep up with monthly payments. Converting a Chapter 7 filing to a Chapter 13 and then back to a Chapter 7 prolongs the debtor's agony.

So the saga continues: Creditors remain unpaid, and even more time passes as the debtor desperately awaits a fresh start. It is true that the harassing collection calls have stopped, but the debtor is no better off financially than before the initial petition filing. It seems, then, that having to jump through the hoops of the means test impedes the debtor's ability to obtain a fresh financial start.

One of the arguments for imposing a means test was to encourage debtors to file under Chapter 13 instead of Chapter 7. Experts thought this would assure that creditors recovered most of the money owed to them. However, the bankruptcy provisions include no real incentive for the debtor to file under Chapter 13. As bankruptcy reform continues, experts should consider including incentives such as reducing the amount of time that a Chapter 13 stays on the debtor's credit report. Currently, a bankruptcy filing can remain on the debtor's credit report for up to 10 years, although some credit-reporting agencies may remove it after 7 years. During that time, it might be harder to obtain a credit card at a favorable rate, to buy a car, to rent an apartment, to qualify for a student loan, or even to get a job.

Chapter 13 debtors exercise discipline, and sometimes sacrifice, in order to pay outstanding debts under their repayment plans. Since they have been under the supervision of a bankruptcy trustee during the repayment plan, permitting the bankruptcy discharge to remain on their credit reports for another 10 years can be considered punishment for seeking bankruptcy protection in the first place. Debtors would be more likely to opt first for Chapter 13 instead of Chapter 7 if they knew they would have a clean slate after successfully completing the repayment plan. The Chapter 13 debtor deserves the opportunity for a meaningful fresh start.

Discharge can be delayed after the Chapter 13 plan is completed.

At the conclusion of the bankruptcy process, the debtor receives what is called a *discharge*. The discharge is the court order that releases the debtor from personal liability for debts that were listed in the bankruptcy petition. It is a central principle under federal bankruptcy law and is essential to the "fresh start" that debtors are afforded after filing for bankruptcy. The debtor will automatically receive a discharge unless there is litigation objecting to it.

The timing of the discharge varies, depending on the chapter under which the case is filed. In a Chapter 7 case, for example, the court usually grants the discharge about four months after the date on which the debtor files the petition. In a typical Chapter 13 case, the court grants the discharge as soon as possible after the debtor completes all payments under the plan. This seldom occurs until about four years after the date of the filing. Thus, under Chapter 13, the debtor's fresh start does not begin until three to five years after they file, and only once the repayment plan has been completed.

Indeed, many debtors choose Chapter 7 over Chapter 13 because of the risk that they will not get a discharge if they cannot make the payments. That is why some consumer advocates contend that debtors who file under Chapter 13 should receive immediate relief, especially when there are no claims to any of

Terms and Concepts

The *bankruptcy discharge* is the court order that releases the debtor from personal liability for *dischargeable debts*. A dischargeable debt is one that is wiped out at the conclusion of the bankruptcy case, unless the judge decides that it should not be. Not all debts are discharged, in which case, the debtor must still repay *nondischargeable debts*. These debts include, but are not limited to, the following: student loans, child support, alimony/maintenance, government fines or penalties, and some taxes. Congress has determined that these types of debts are not dischargeable for public policy reasons—based either on the nature of the debt or the fact that the debts were incurred due to the improper behavior of the debtor, such as fines for drunk driving.

their property or other secured assets involved. This would certainly be an incentive for debtors to file under Chapter 13 instead of under Chapter 7.

Even after struggling through the arduous Chapter 13 process, there are events that could delay the final discharge. The most common delay occurs when the debtor is not able to make the scheduled payments. If this happens, the case is either dismissed or the Chapter 13 filing is converted to a Chapter 7. If the Chapter 13 filing is dismissed, the debtor receives no discharge. If the case is converted, the debtor normally incurs additional attorneys' fees and filing fees, must file new schedules and statements, and must attend a new meeting of creditors.

Statistics on Bankruptcy Laws

- The number of bankruptcies is approaching two million per year, which is about six times as many as were filed in 1980, and twice as many as in 1995. In other words, the number of bankruptcy filings has increased by more than 100 percent over the last 10 years.
- Ninety percent of bankruptcies are caused by unemployment, medical bills, or divorce. The remaining 10 percent are caused by other factors, such as business failure, overuse of credit cards, etc.
- Household debt is at a record high relative to disposable income.
- One-third of bankruptcy filers owe more than a year's salary on credit cards alone.
- In 2006, approximately 150 million Americans had credit cards, including college and high school students—80 percent more than 15 years ago.
- The dollar amount of credit card debt grew about 350 percent over the same period. This does not include mortgage debt, student loans, and automobile loans.

There are other times, too, when the bankruptcy discharge is delayed even though the debtor has completed the repayment plan. The delay can be caused by the following events:

The debtor does not complete an instructional course on personal financial management. The court may deny an individual debtor's discharge in a Chapter 7 or Chapter 13 case if the debtor fails to complete "an instructional course concerning financial management." The new mandate is very similar to the consumer credit counseling required before filing a petition. The bankruptcy court may waive this requirement only if there are inadequate educational programs available, or the debtor is disabled, incapacitated, or on active military duty in a combat zone.

The debtor does not produce evidence that all tax returns were filed while the Chapter 13 case was pending. Under the new law, if debtors fail to file a return that becomes due after the date of their bankruptcy petition, or fail to file for an extension, the Internal Revenue Service (IRS) may request the court to order a conversion (a change from Chapter 7 to Chapter 11, or from Chapter 11 to Chapter 13, for example) or a dismissal of the case. In addition, debtors must also provide a copy of the tax return or transcript to requesting creditors, which can further delay the final discharge order.

The debtor does not certify that all past and post-filing domestic support obligations have been paid in full or are current. A debtor who is required to pay child support or alimony under a domestic support order (DSO) must file a certification with the court that all DSO payments are current before receiving a discharge.

Increases in attorneys' fees impede access to the system.

The new bankruptcy act has made filing bankruptcy petitions more complicated and confusing. Far more paperwork is required than under the old law. As a result, bankruptcy filers are now paying much higher fees: Bankruptcy attorneys have raised their fees by as much as 100 percent,[2] justifying the increase by saying they have to do far more work for each case than they did under the old law.

In October 2006, the National Association of Consumer Bankruptcy Attorneys released the results of its bankruptcy law anniversary survey. Of the 700 members surveyed, more than 75 percent said that it now takes at least 50 percent more time than before to prepare a bankruptcy filing.[3]

The high cost of attorneys' fees has a chilling effect on the number of debtors who seek bankruptcy protection. Because they cannot afford an attorney's advice when the situation arises, they delay action until they are even deeper in debt and have no real alternatives. A 2006 eMediaWire press release explains the absurdity of this result: "Bankruptcy is a federal program established by Congress to provide debt relief to people who need it. The program was not intended to cost hundreds or thousands of dollars in attorney fees. It simply makes no sense that those individuals who are unable to pay their current debts would have the ability to pay $800 to $2,500 in attorney fees to file bankruptcy."[4]

Not only must attorneys have to file more paperwork than ever, the new law also requires them to verify the accuracy of their clients' financial information before filing. If the information is wrong, the bankruptcy attorney can be held responsible. The American Bar Association has strongly opposed the increased liability, as well as other new provisions "that dramatically increase the liability and administrative burdens of bankruptcy attorneys while denying effective legal representation" to consumers who seek bankruptcy protection.[5] Many attorneys are not willing to take on this added responsibility and stop practicing bankruptcy law. This, of course, greatly reduces the pool of available, experienced attorneys.

Even more disheartening is that 93 percent of the bankruptcy attorneys surveyed also reported that the increased paperwork has not changed the outcome of bankruptcy filings. Rather, it has merely increased the costs of the process.[6] In other words, there is no evidence that bankruptcy reform has reduced abuse of the bankruptcy system. All it does is discourage debtors from seeking much needed relief.

Summary

Credit card companies and other supporters declared the Bankruptcy Abuse Prevention and Consumer Protection Act of 2005 (BAPCPA) a success by the end of its first year. Because consumers now must pass a means test, fewer Chapter 7 bankruptcies were being filed. This provides an opportunity for creditors to receive payments under the Chapter 13 repayment plan. Bankruptcy attorneys and other consumer advocates, however, say that the provisions are too stringent and make it too difficult for debtors to get a fresh start. Indeed, even if a debtor fails the means test by $1, he or she is forced to file under Chapter 13. The only alternative is not to file at all.

It is true that creditors are prohibited from harassing debtors during the three- to five-year repayment plan period, but the debts have yet to be discharged. Moreover, debtors are concerned that they will not be able to make the payments under the Chapter 13 repayment plan without a change in their current income. If that happens, their bankruptcy might be converted to a Chapter 7, freeing them from the payments. In the meantime, however, they still have not received a discharge and the outstanding amounts remain due.

The new provisions also impose burdensome responsibilities on attorneys. For example, attorneys must now ensure the accuracy of the information included in the bankruptcy petition.[7] Under the old law, the debtor was responsible for accurately reporting information concerning debts and income. Many bankruptcy attorneys reportedly now spend much more time on a typical bankruptcy case than they did in the past. As a result, they are demanding to be paid for the extra work. It is no wonder that greater numbers of debtors are attempting to file bankruptcy petitions without the assistance of an attorney.

Unfortunately, the filing requirements are so complex that bankruptcy courts often reject these filings and, once again, debtors miss the opportunity to get a fresh start through bankruptcy protection. They simply cannot afford it.

Mandatory Credit Counseling Benefits Consumers and Lenders

> Bankruptcy is one of those words, like war, that you have heard all of your life and think that you understand until you actually become involved with the process the word is intended to identify.
>
> —Jerome Weidman, *Fourth Street East*, 1970

Perhaps you have seen those television commercials about people drowning in debt. The continuous collection calls and letters are driving them crazy. They need relief. By calling a 1-800 number, they can reduce or eliminate their debt, stop the harassing collection activities, clean up their credit report, and get back on the path to financial stability. All with one, low monthly payment! As the scene fades, a satisfied, smiling husband and wife relax on their backyard patio, each sipping a glass of lemonade. Again, the toll-free number flashes across the bottom of the screen, with the name of a consumer credit counseling agency promising to take care of all debts.

Mandatory credit counseling is key to bankruptcy reform.

Under the new provisions of BAPCPA, a debtor must get budget and credit counseling within 180 days before filing for bankruptcy. Consumer credit counselors advise debtors to file for bankruptcy only as a last resort and give debtors the opportunity to explore alternatives. This results in fewer bankruptcy filings, in debtors reducing their debt in a more methodical way, and in creditors being repaid. Ultimately, it leads to better-informed money managers who can make better financial (spending and saving) decisions.

Supporters of bankruptcy reform say credit counseling gets debtors back on track. A credit counseling service can also help negotiate better interest rates that are within the debtor's budget. Creditors are open to these negotiations because they realize that they are better off receiving a percentage of the original obligation than receiving no payments at all.

Steve Bartlett, president and CEO of the Financial Services Roundtable,[1] argues that consumer credit counseling services play an important role in making consumers more financially fit:

> The Roundtable is encouraged by the results of the [National Foundation for Credit Counseling] study showing that "poor money management" (66.9 percent) is the top reason consumers go through bankruptcy. This is consistent with our "Financial Fitness" poll, which found that the more likely people are to seek financial advice, the better chance their finances will be in excellent shape long-term.
>
> The results of the Roundtable's survey show that 84 percent of Americans believe they are in excellent or okay financial fitness shape. Of that group, half of them had received

> outside financial advice. Conversely, only 1 in 10 who felt they were in terrible financial shape had sought outside financial advice. Therefore, you can conclude that financial advice for consumers equates to a better understanding of finances, which results in better money management and fewer bankruptcies.[2]

Consumer credit counselors can also help the debtor develop a more formal debt management plan (DMP). Under a DMP, the debtor agrees to cut up credit cards and promises not to incur more debt. The debtor makes a fixed monthly payment to the

National Foundation for Credit Counseling Applauds U.S. Trustees for Setting High Standards in Approval Process

Executive Office Releases Application and Approval Process for Non-profit Organizations

Silver Spring, Md.—On Tuesday, the Executive Office for U.S. Trustees began accepting applications for approval as a budget and credit counseling agency and/or provider of financial education. Approved organizations will provide the pre-filing counseling and predischarge education mandated by the Bankruptcy Abuse Prevention and Consumer Protection Act of 2005. This is the first major announcement made by the Executive Office since Bankruptcy Reform was signed into law earlier this year. "The criteria set forth by the Executive Office reflects a very strong commitment on their part to ensure that the counseling and education provisions are substantive in nature and of the highest quality," Susan C. Keating, President and CEO of the National Foundation for Credit Counseling (NFCC). "The NFCC shares in the Executive Office's vision to provide the consumer with the most effective and comprehensive counseling and education available."

Source: Excerpt from NFCC Press Release (July 7, 2005). Available online at http://www.nfcc.org/bankruptcy/index.cfm.

credit counseling agency, which distributes the money to various creditors according to the DMP. The agency uses the deposits to pay unsecured debts, such as credit card bills, student loans, and medical bills. The monthly payment includes a small administrative fee that the credit counseling agency keeps.

By obtaining a few hours or a few weeks of credit counseling, the debtor will develop a debt reduction plan and possibly an effective savings plan. Although some may see this requirement as an embarrassing exposure of a personal financial crisis, it is far less embarrassing than having a bankruptcy on one's credit record for 10 years.

Credit counseling agencies are approved by the U.S. Trustees Office.

The credit counseling industry has been under attack over the past several years because of allegations of unscrupulous business practices. Many people believe that the agencies take advantage of desperate consumers seeking help. Some of these agencies have also been accused of engaging in deceptive trade practices, charging excessive fees, and forcing debtors into formal repayment plans even when it was not in the debtors' best interest to do so.[3]

Since credit counseling plays a vital role in helping consumers recover from financial difficulties, only reputable, responsible agencies should be allowed to provide counseling. The new bankruptcy laws have a built-in safeguard to protect consumers from unscrupulous agencies. Under section 111 of the new law, the bankruptcy court clerk must maintain a public list of consumer credit counseling agencies that the U.S. Trustees Office has approved. This government stamp of approval assures the public that these agencies are legitimate and operate for the benefit of the consumer. To be included on the approved list, the counseling agency must meet certain standards: For example, the U.S. Trustees Office requires each agency to show that it "will provide qualified counselors, maintain adequate provision for safekeeping and payment of client funds, provide adequate counseling with respect to client credit problems, and deal effectively with other matters relating to the quality, effectiveness, and financial security of the services it provides."[4] Credit counseling agencies must also meet a number of specific criteria regarding the management of their finances, as well as the types of financial incentives they provide to their counselors.

To demonstrate their commitment to providing quality services, agencies must also receive industry accreditation from a reputable credit counseling organization. Industry accreditation organizations impose strict standards on their member agencies and serve as industry watchdogs against unscrupulous behavior. One such organization is the National Foundation for Credit Counseling (NFCC), the nation's largest and oldest national nonprofit credit counseling organization.

The credit counseling requirement is applied fairly.

The legislative intent in requiring debtors to obtain pre-petition credit counseling was to give potential filers "an opportunity to learn about the consequences of bankruptcy . . . before they decide to file for bankruptcy relief."[5] Opponents of the 2005 bankruptcy law argue that this is a burdensome requirement that merely delays the filing process. They claim that Congress's real intent was to discourage people from filing.

Congress recognized that circumstances might exist that would make it unfair or even impossible for a debtor to obtain the required counseling. It was clear that this requirement must be applied with some flexibility to allow for special circumstances. Accordingly, on October 4, 2005, the Executive Office of the U.S. Trustee temporarily waived the credit counseling requirement for bankruptcy filers in Louisiana and the Southern District of Mississippi because of Hurricane Katrina.

Congress also included provisions in the new bankruptcy laws to allow courts, after notice and a hearing, either to excuse the debtor from the requirement or to extend the amount of time allowed the debtor to complete the counseling. The court determines whether an extension or a waiver is appropriate, based on

The Facts of *In re Tulper*

In *In re Tulper*, 345 B.R. 322, (Bankr. D. Col. 2006), the court granted the debtor's Motion for Waiver of Budget and Credit Counseling. At the evidentiary hearing, the court found that Mrs. Tulper, age 60, suffered from heart problems, tremors, asthma, a bad lung, arthritis, a disintegrated spine, and a plate in her right ankle, which combined to make her wheelchair-bound. Moreover, Mrs. Tulper was taking approximately 17 prescribed medications, which she brought to the hearing in their regular container that "was the size of a small tool box." . . . The court also found that Mr. Tulper, age 81, who was Mrs. Tulper's care giver, could not hear or had little hearing capability even with the use of a hearing aid. He also had 40% disability with respect to use of hands and feet. Neither of them had any computer skills.

The court found that there are three elements required to satisfy the disability requirement: (1) the debtor is severely physically impaired; (2) the debtor has made a reasonable effort, despite the impairment, to participate in the pre-petition credit counseling; and (3) the debtor is unable, because of the impairment, to participate meaningfully in an in person, telephone, or Internet briefing pre-petition. The court easily found that the debtors were physically impaired. The debtors also made a reasonable effort to address credit counseling by conferring with their accountant and attorney, who found that it was very difficult to communicate anything with the debtors. The court found that the Tulpers could not meaningfully participate in the briefing because of their communication difficulties.

Thus, the purpose of counseling could not be fulfilled, and the requirement would be waived: "If a debtor goes to credit counseling and, because of a significant impairment, cannot participate in the credit counseling such that he or she can understand what is conveyed during the credit counseling session, so as to be able to have the 'opportunity to learn about the consequences of bankruptcy,' then the prepetition credit counseling becomes meaningless."

Source: Daniel Cervantes, "Incapacity and Disability Waivers for Credit Counseling Explored," ABI's BAPCPA Blog. http://bapcpa.blogspot.com/2006/07/incapacity-and-disability-waivers-for.html (July 23, 2006).

the debtor's particular circumstances. A waiver may be granted in three cases:

- No approved counseling services exist in the debtor's area.
- The individual files a certification with the court establishing that either

  (a) difficult circumstances merit a waiver of pre-petition credit counseling, or

  (b) the individual requested, but was unable to receive, credit counseling within five days of the request

  and the court is satisfied with the certification.
- The debtor is either incapacitated, disabled, or on active military duty in a combat zone.[6]

Although there are no other exceptions to the pre-petition credit counseling requirement, courts have broadly interpreted what constitutes "difficult circumstances."[7]

Courts have excused debtors from mandatory counseling when the debtor could not meaningfully participate because of communication difficulties. One court concluded that if a debtor goes to credit counseling and, because of a significant impairment, cannot understand what is conveyed during the credit counseling session, then the pre-petition credit counseling becomes meaningless.[8] Similarly, a court held that the credit counseling requirement could not be imposed on a debtor who had very limited English-speaking ability, and when no approved agency had counselors who spoke the debtor's language.[9]

Summary

Consumer credit counseling is considered a key factor in bankruptcy reform and is beneficial to both the consumer and the creditor. Counseling provides consumers an opportunity to consider alternatives to bankruptcy and to better understand and manage their personal finances. The result is that fewer bankruptcies are filed, creditors are repaid, and debtors are more stable financially. Because of the critical role that credit counseling agencies play in helping the debtor to recover, debtors should only use services of credit counseling agencies that have been approved by the U.S. Trustee's Office.

Although it may be somewhat inconvenient to attend, credit counseling is time well spent. After all, isn't financial recovery the goal for the debtor? Without financial management training, debtors will quickly slip back into the poor financial habits that got them into trouble in the first place.

Consumer Credit Counseling Is Counterproductive and Subject to Fraud

Credit counseling is a burden to the consumer and impedes relief.

One of the purposes of the bankruptcy reform is to reduce the number of Chapter 7 bankruptcy filings, especially those in which consumers repeatedly file in order to avoid repaying debts. These "serial filers" continue to incur debt with no intention of repaying their bills. In an effort to combat this type of behavior, Congress added a requirement to the new law that consumers must participate in consumer credit counseling within 180 days before filing a bankruptcy petition. The goal of the pre-petition counseling requirement is to educate consumers about alternatives to bankruptcy and to determine if there is another way to relieve their financial distress. The pre-petition counseling requirement is imposed not only on repeat filers but on any person who desires bankruptcy protection.

Bankruptcy courts have full discretion to determine whether bankruptcy filing fees can be waived. The courts make this determination on a case-by-case basis, depending on the debtor's particular circumstances. For example, a New Hampshire court determined that the debtors qualified for a waiver of bankruptcy filing fees because of the severity of their financial hardship but still required them to obtain pre-petition counseling.

Many people think it is counterproductive to require debtors to seek counseling and explore alternatives to bankruptcy when they are already in dire financial straits and cannot even afford to pay the bankruptcy filing fees. If the debtors qualify for a waiver of the filing fees, then they probably cannot pay their debts and, therefore, need bankruptcy protection. Judge J. Michael Deasy, a bankruptcy judge in New Hampshire, raised these same concerns in a 2006 case. Judge Deasy pointed out that "[i]t is a mystery . . . why Congress granted the Court the authority to waive all filing fees . . . but not waive the credit counseling requirement. . . . Exactly what form of credit counseling could be useful, or necessary, to a person who qualifies for waiver of fees . . . is even more of a mystery."[1]

A bankruptcy court in Florida did find that certain circumstances may justify a waiver of the counseling requirement. In one case, a creditor had frozen the debtor's bank account, which was his only source of income. The court held that this situation justified a waiver of the pre-petition credit counseling requirement because the debtor had no access to his funds.[2]

Under the current law, if a debtor does not participate in credit counseling prior to filing the bankruptcy petition, he or she is denied bankruptcy relief. Although credit counseling may be beneficial to the debtor during the financial recovery process, requiring counseling prior to filing merely adds to the debtor's financial distress.

Some credit counseling agencies are scam operations.

Legitimate consumer credit counseling agencies provide a valuable service to consumers who are seeking alternatives to bankruptcy. Unfortunately, many of these so-called "nonprofit" agencies engage in unscrupulous practices that ultimately worsen the consumer's financial situation.

Consider the following hypothetical situation, for example: Samantha's ex-husband was addicted to shopping and amassed an extraordinary amount of credit card and "easy installment payment" debt during the early years of their marriage. They were unable to keep up with the payments and were at least 60 days behind on all their credit card bills. They considered bankruptcy, but then discovered an ad from a nonprofit credit counseling agency that promised to stop the harassing debt collection calls and to help them consolidate their debt into one low, monthly payment.

They contacted the agency and immediately entered into a debt management plan (DMP). They agreed to pay the agency $450 each month, which the agency would distribute among the couple's creditors. But two months later, when applying for a home mortgage, they discovered that most of the creditors had neither been paid nor even been contacted to make payment arrangements. Instead of distributing the monthly payment according to the DMP, the credit counseling agency kept a portion of the money as a monthly administrative fee and made late payments or, in some instances, no payments at all. The stress was a contributing cause of the couple's divorce, and neither of them recovered financially. Although they thought they were moving in the right direction by entering into a DMP, they found themselves in an even worse credit position than before. They would have been better off had they paid the $900 directly to their creditors during those two months.

Consumer credit counseling can be an effective tool in helping debtors through difficult financial situations, but only if the services are provided by legitimate agencies. The credit counseling industry has had a questionable reputation over the years. The National Consumer Law Center and the Consumer Federation of America released a report in 2003 that highlighted some of the key problems in the industry.[3]

One major problem is the deceptive and misleading practices perpetuated by certain agencies, some of which do not pay the consumers' DMP payments on time and do not disclose administrative fees to consumers.

The second issue concerns excessive costs: A credit counseling agency's revenue is generated through an administrative fee paid by the debtor, as well as a fee for the educational component that the agency offers. Historically, creditors also made substantial donations to cover a portion of debtors' costs—acceptable, since creditors have a real interest in helping debtors become financially stable—and these donations added to the agency's revenue. Yet these "fair share" contributions, which are usually calculated as a percentage of the debtor's balance with the creditor, have dwindled over the years. When creditors realized how much they were paying consumer credit counseling agencies for "fair share" contributions, they increased their scrutiny of these agencies. Creditors now contend that many of the agencies that have entered the market do very little counseling, charge consumers high fees, and recommend DMPs without regard for a customer's individual circumstances. Creditors are concerned that DMPs initiated by these newer agencies are often based only on 15-minute phone conversations and have a significantly reduced chance of success. In response to the decreasing success of DMPs, some credit card issuers are offering lower fair share contributions, or in some cases, no contributions at all.[4] Traditionally, creditors contributed about 15 percent of the funds that agencies collected from their customers. By 1999, the contribution level had decreased to 9 percent. In 2002, some credit card issuers reported contribution levels as low as three percent to zero percent.[5] Because creditors have reduced their funding, it is reasonable to expect an increase in the fee that the consumer pays, but some agencies charge as much as a full month's consolidated DMP payment simply to establish an account. Fees that high are not justified.

In addition, some "nonprofit" credit counseling agencies perform like regular, for-profit business enterprises while reaping the benefits of having a nonprofit status. The Internal Revenue Service (IRS) released a report in 2006 that explains its concerns about this. According to the report, "credit counseling agencies were [traditionally] non-profit organizations that relied on contributions and small fees from consumers to cover the operating costs of providing advice, debt counseling, and limited debt management plans to consumers who had trouble paying their credit card bills."[6] These agencies were exempt from paying taxes because they guaranteed to provide educational and counseling services to debtors in need. The services were not meant to be financially profitable to the agency.

Over the years, however, many credit counseling organizations changed their business strategies to focus their efforts on selling debt management plans. According to the IRS report, these arrangements are motivated by profit and offer little or no counseling or education. Moreover, in many cases, the credit counseling organizations also serve the private interests of related for-profit businesses, officers, and directors. Since the law now requires the U.S. Trustee to scrutinize credit counseling services, some of these agencies have been identified and shut down before they could do harm to pre-bankruptcy consumers. Still, however, there have been problems. AmeriDebt, headed by Andris Pukke, is a prime example.[7]

AmeriDebt deceived consumers by presenting itself as a nonprofit organization while taking profits from its customers and giving them to its for-profit business partners. In addition to that, the Federal Trade Commission (FTC) reported that AmeriDebt failed to counsel consumers in debt management as advertised. Instead, it put every customer in a debt management plan. Under a legitimate DMP, the consumer pays a flat, monthly amount to the credit counseling agency, which is then distributed among the consumer's creditors in accordance with terms that have been negotiated on the consumer's behalf. The FTC further charged that AmeriDebt deceived customers by claiming to offer services with no start-up fee. This was not the case, the

FTC said. AmeriDebt reportedly kept its clients' first DMP payment as a start-up instead of using it to pay creditors. This deception put the debtors further behind on payments and deeper into financial trouble. The complaint against AmeriDebt was filed in November 2003 and charged that these practices were deceptive in violation of the Federal Trade Commission Act.

AmeriDebt filed for bankruptcy itself the summer after the FTC complaint was filed. The FTC asked the bankruptcy court to remove AmeriDebt's head officers from their positions and to appoint a trustee to oversee the company. The court obliged, and in March 2005, AmeriDebt agreed to shut down its debt management operations and settled the other FTC charges. About a year and a half later, the FTC and Andris Pukke finalized a settlement in which Pukke gave nearly all of his assets—possibly up to $35 million—to the people whom the company had hurt.[8]

Although this case was eventually settled, more than 300,000 consumers had been adversely affected before the FTC discovered the scam.[9] Obviously, only strict oversight can provide real protection against this kind of deception by seemingly legitimate credit counseling agencies. Many consumers continue to make monthly payments to their credit counseling agency and only discover that their payments were not turned over to their creditors as laid out in their DMP when they begin to receive calls and letters from collection agencies. They might also discover the deception when they apply for a home mortgage and see that their credit score is much lower than it was before they sought counseling. The last thing that bankruptcy-bound consumers need is for an agency to take advantage of them through a credit repair or credit counseling scam.

There is no evidence that pre-petition counseling is effective.

In 2005, when it became apparent that there would be changes in the laws governing bankruptcy, debtors rushed to file bankruptcy petitions. Most believed that it would be virtually impossible to obtain bankruptcy protection after the new provisions passed. Consumers would need to show that they were unable to pay their debts, would have to pay higher fees, file reams of paperwork, and satisfy other complicated and unreasonable pre-filing requirements. Thus, in the 16 days before the new law took effect, consumers filed more than 600,000 bankruptcy cases—roughly 40 percent of a typical year's cases.

In early 2006, after the changes in the law went in effect, the number of filings plummeted. Bankruptcy reform supporters argued that this dramatic decrease demonstrated the effectiveness of the new law and suggested that debtors were finding alternatives to bankruptcy to address their financial situations. Many thought this meant that pre-petition consumer credit counseling was working.

There is no evidence, however, to support this view. In fact, the early 2006 decrease in the number of filings was misleading due to the unusually large number of pre-reform filings in 2005 noted above. Arguably, some of these consumers would have filed in 2006 if it weren't for the new laws. Although they might still have filed in 2006, the number of filings would have been distributed at normal levels.

Furthermore, a decreased number of filings is no proof that people sought different means to solve financial crises. When faced with the challenge of figuring out the new bankruptcy process and additional restrictions, it is understandable that debtors would avoid, or at least delay, bankruptcy. Avoiding the process, however, does not necessarily mean that a debtor took care of a financial crisis through alternative means. Rather, it could mean that he or she continued to struggle hopelessly with the situation without relief.

Since the initial decrease in filings in early 2006, the number of consumer bankruptcy filings has continued to rise. According to the American Bankruptcy Institute, this number increased by 40 percent in 2007. A Detroit newspaper reported that through October 2007, the number of Chapter 7 bankruptcies filed in the Eastern District of Michigan alone jumped 63 percent compared to the first 10 months of 2006.[10]

Although Michigan's economy is among the worst in the nation, there is a pattern of increasing numbers of filings in other states, as well. On March 10, 2008, an Iowa newspaper reported that the number of consumer bankruptcies filed in Iowa increased from 4,500 in 2006 to 6,700 in 2007—a 48 percent increase.[11] Ohio reported a 43 percent increase in the number of consumer bankruptcy filings from 2006 to 2007. On January 3, 2008, the American Bankruptcy Institute reported that U.S. consumer bankruptcy filings increased nearly 40 percent nationwide from 2006 to 2007. This steady increase in filings proves that pre-petition counseling is not effective. Evidently, the credit counselors have failed to convince consumers that there are meaningful alternatives to bankruptcy.

Summary

While it is true that legitimate consumer credit counseling agencies can provide a valuable service to consumers who are seeking financial recovery, requiring debtors to participate in counseling prior to filing a bankruptcy petition is ineffective. Such a requirement merely acts as a barrier for debtors who need immediate bankruptcy relief. Debtors may be unaware of the counseling requirement or simply unable to afford the services. In any event, having to get counseling prior to filing a bankruptcy petition adds to the already burdensome situation of having to file in the first place.

Far too many of these agencies are scam operations that leave debtors worse off than they were before participating in credit counseling. Credit counselors generally have no more power to negotiate with creditors than debtors do. Moreover, some credit counselors receive a percentage of or commission on whatever the creditors receive. Thus, it is in the credit counselor's best interest to make sure the debtor pays as much as he or she can possibly afford, even if the payments put greater financial strain on the debtor and his or her family. Time has shown that, after going through rigorous credit counseling, most people eventually end up filing for bankruptcy anyway.

Bankruptcy Laws Allow People to Rebuild Their Finances Responsibly

> One of the primary purposes of the Bankruptcy Act is to relieve the honest debtor from the weight of oppressive indebtedness.
>
> —*Williams v. U.S. Fidelity & Guar. Co.*, 1915

Debtors still get a fresh financial start under new bankruptcy provisions.

One of the long-standing principles behind bankruptcy discharge is that it provides debtors with a fresh start and an opportunity for financial recovery. It is true that bankruptcy eliminates some debts, and also stops collection calls and letters. Some Chapter 13 filers get to keep their homes and cars if they can stay current with the payments. And yet, they might not be in better financial condition than they were before declaring bankruptcy. So, does bankruptcy give debtors a fresh start? What really happens to families after bankruptcy?

In early 2006, Katherine A. Porter and Deborah Thorne conducted a study of how people were doing one year after receiving a Chapter 7 bankruptcy discharge.[1] The subject families were asked whether their financial situations had "improved," "stayed about the same," or "worsened." Porter and Thorne reported their findings that:

> . . . the majority, 65 percent of families, reported that their financial situations had improved since they filed bankruptcy. The Chapter 7 discharge appears to have worked effectively to reduce or eliminate the hardship facing these families. Free from most past debts, these families are able to concentrate their future income on ongoing expenses rather than struggling with overwhelming old debt. . . . From these data, it appears that approximately 2 in 3 families have achieved a meaningful fresh start after bankruptcy and are on the road to financial health.[2]

This is good news for the American family. It is, after all, one of the primary reasons that the bankruptcy system was established. Bankruptcy lifts the heavy burden of financial distress from the shoulders of hard-working consumers. Now they can begin to rebuild their finances in a responsible way without the stress of collection calls and letters, and without the constant guilty feelings associated with the inability to pay their debts.

Debtors seek alternatives to bankruptcy thanks to reforms.

Prior to the BAPCPA in 2005, the bankruptcy code did not provide for financial education as a condition to a bankruptcy filing. Consumers came out of bankruptcy with the same spending habits and money management skills that they had when they went into bankruptcy. According to a survey released in October 2006, testing by some credit counseling agencies shows that consumers improve their financial knowledge by 10 to 40 percent, at least in the short term, because of counseling.[3]

Even though bankruptcy filings have increased drastically over the past three decades, debtors are still advised to file for bankruptcy only as a last resort. There are other ways to survive financial crises, among which are the following alternatives:

Do nothing. This may be appropriate for debts that are small or where the debtor is elderly or "judgment proof." To be judgment proof simply means that you have so little money and own so little property that you would not be able to pay a court judgment entered against you. Even if a creditor sues you and wins, you are no worse off than you were before. After all, creditors cannot get money from you if you do not have any money. You can also stop the annoying collection phone calls and letters without filing for bankruptcy. Under the federal Fair Debt Collections Practices Act,[4] you can legally demand that collection agencies stop contacting you—even if you really do owe them.

Negotiate with creditors. This might be a good alternative for debtors who have income available. It may also buy them some time until their financial situation improves. Creditors who believe that a debtor really wants to pay off debts may be willing to reduce the payments, extend the time to pay, or excuse the late fees and penalties that have accrued. They are often willing to settle on debts for a percentage of the balance due if the debts have been delinquent for several months. Creditors sometimes settle for as little as 40 percent of the total amount due. One of the pitfalls of settling, however, is that the creditor often requires that the settlement be paid in one lump sum. There also may be tax consequences because the IRS sometimes views the forgiven debt as income to the debtor.

Make a debt management plan. A debtor can seek consumer credit counseling services even if he or she is not considering bankruptcy. It is still a wise idea to select an agency from the U.S. Trustee's pre-approved list. A credit counselor can help a person design a debt management plan (DMP) and might be able to negotiate better terms on debt repayment. The disadvantage of choosing this approach is that the DMP operates in almost the same way as a Chapter 13 repayment plan. A debtor makes one lump-sum payment each month to the credit counseling agency that then distributes the payments to creditors. The advantage of this is that no bankruptcy will appear on the person's credit report.

These approaches may be viable options for some debtors, but others conclude that bankruptcy is the only way they can recover.

Bankruptcy reform influences the borrowing and spending habits of American families.

Prior to the 2005 bankruptcy law, it was easy to file for bankruptcy. The debtor could decide whether to file under Chapter 7 or Chapter 13 or both. There was no means test to satisfy, and no requirement to seek credit counseling before filing. The only real barrier was whether or not the consumer was willing to deal with the stigma of bankruptcy. Prior to bankruptcy reform, debtors who filed for bankruptcy were stigmatized in that their bankruptcy record adversely affected their ability to obtain credit or sometimes even to find employment. This effectively barred debtors from participating in certain areas of society. By 2005, however, some debtors were no longer concerned about the stigma because bankruptcy was fairly common, even among the rich and famous. It had become more socially acceptable, no longer a label to be feared.

In referring to the pre-BAPCPA bankruptcy laws, Judge Edith Jones of the National Bankruptcy Review Commission noted in congressional testimony that the social stigma associated with the old system of bankruptcy law no longer exists:

> At one time in our history, filing bankruptcy was regarded as shameful, and filers suffered social stigma and permanently ruined credit. The shame and stigma are no longer compelling. . . . [M]any filers now commence cases without ever having been in default on their debts. This suggests that bankruptcy is, to them, not a last resort but a first resort. Many debtors are well-off and continue to be fully employed before and after filing bankruptcy. Lawyer advertising, do-it-yourself kits, and bankruptcy mills expand the pool of potential filers. Well-publicized celebrity bankruptcies, plus "water cooler" gossip about increasing filings, have tended to reduce bankruptcy to an acceptable alternative for personal financial management.[5]

Summary

Prior to the BAPCPA, the apparent ease of bankruptcy coupled with the lessened stigma of it influenced Americans' spending and borrowing habits. In other words, Americans spent freely because they did not fear the consequences of debt. The only thing that kept a debtor from filing was his or her own conscience. With the new law, American consumers are becoming more aware that bankruptcy is not an acceptable way to handle debt. Consumers are also realizing that bankruptcy can have a negative impact on a family's financial situation for many, many years. It will take a long time for public perception to change, but in the meantime, bankruptcy reform will continue to influence spending and borrowing habits and will reduce the number of people who turn to bankruptcy.

Bankruptcy Reforms Do Not Solve the Real Problem for Millions of Americans

Debtors continue to struggle to take care of basic expenses.

Even when a debtor obtains a bankruptcy discharge, he or she is likely to be no better off than before filing. Take one couple, Steve and Carol, for example: The parents of two small children, both with college business degrees, had been married for five years when their financial troubles hit. Carol was laid off from her job in the marketing department of a local car manufacturing plant. The year after that, the company that Steve worked for closed its doors. With both parents unemployed, it was a very difficult time for the family. They had no choice but to file for bankruptcy. Although they were hopeful for the future after receiving the Chapter 7 discharge, another six months passed and neither of them found full-time employment. In the meantime, they continued to get further behind on their mortgage and utility payments. Clearly, there was no "fresh start" for Steve and Carol.

Steve and Carol's plight is not unusual. Many families find themselves in similar circumstances after going through the bankruptcy process. A 2006 study examined data related to the financial condition of families one year after receiving a bankruptcy discharge. The results of this study demonstrated that a steady and sufficient income is key to improving financial stability after bankruptcy—relief from immediate debts is not enough. The researchers concluded that, for many families,

> . . . the fresh start either never materialized or quickly went stale. Instead, the bankruptcy discharge signaled little more than the beginning of another long period of trying—but apparently failing—to make ends meet. Bankruptcy certainly reduced these families' total debt levels and provided a temporary reprieve from creditor pressures. However, the bankruptcy discharge did not produce lasting financial relief.[1]

Even two years after the 2005 bankruptcy law went into effect, there was little evidence that people who have filed for bankruptcy can better manage their money or deal with a financial crisis. Rather than providing a fresh start, it seems that bankruptcy merely provides a short break from financial stress. Families continue to struggle even after old debts have been discharged. Perhaps the real problem is not excessive spending. Perhaps families just fail to generate enough income to take care of their basic needs. A family that must use credit to cover the costs of groceries and heating will always be in financial crisis.

According to Porter and Thorne's 2006 study, one year after bankruptcy discharge, 1 in 4 debtors was struggling to pay routine bills, and 1 in 3 debtors reported an overall financial situation similar to or worse than when they filed for bankruptcy.[2] In other words, these debtors were not in financial crises because of frivolous spending or credit card misuse. They were struggling to meet basic living expenses—expenses that for most people seldom involve the use of credit.

> The post-bankruptcy expenses that families struggled to pay were mundane. More than one-third of the families reported that it was difficult to pay their monthly utility bills, such as heat, electricity, water, phone, or garbage. Approximately 1 in 3 families struggled with car payments or car repairs. . . . Even more alarming, about one-fourth of families found it hard to make their mortgage or rent payments after bankruptcy. Thus,

2007 Health and Human Services Poverty Guidelines

Persons in Family or Household	48 Contiguous States and D.C.	Alaska	Hawaii
1	$10,210	$12,770	$11,750
2	$13,690	$17,120	$15,750
3	$17,170	$21,470	$19,750
4	$20,650	$25,820	$23,750
5	$24,130	$30,170	$27,750
6	$27,610	$34,520	$31,750
7	$31,090	$38,870	$35,750
8	$34,570	$43,220	$39,750
For each additional person, add	$3,480	$4,350	$4,000

Source: *Federal Register*, Vol. 72, No. 15, January 24, 2007, pp. 3147–3148.

> even without the burden of debt, many post-bankruptcy debtors struggle to meet their families' basic needs.[3]

The study concluded that the lack of steady and sufficient income was the key factor causing these debtors to be worse off or in the same situation as when they filed for bankruptcy:

> Our analysis of these data demonstrates that steady and sufficient income is the key to improved post-bankruptcy financial health. Factors that cause household income to decline, such as unemployment and underemployment, illness or injury, and old age, undermine the chances of financial recovery. These data reveal the limitations of bankruptcy as a social safety net and highlight the fragile economic situations of American families.[4]

Debtors continue to use credit cards.

There are many theories concerning the leading cause for so many consumer bankruptcy filings. Some consider the primary cause to be excessive credit card debt and mismanagement of personal finances. Others contend that consumers see bankruptcy as an opportunity to avoid responsibility with very little consequence. The American Bar Association, however, has reported that about 90 percent of bankruptcies are the result of unemployment, medical bills, or divorce.[5] If a wage earner becomes seriously ill or unemployed, he or she turns to credit cards to get through tough financial times. Only 10 percent of bankruptcies are caused by other events such as business failure or overuse of credit cards.[6]

Despite the risks, there are more than a few companies willing to extend credit to people who have been through the bankruptcy process. Credit lending is a profitable business. According to a survey conducted by the Center for Responsible Lending, credit card debt has tripled since the 1990s. From 2000 to 2005, credit card use increased 31 percent.[7] In an article for *Notre Dame*

Business online magazine, Peter Agostino suggested one reason for this change: "Many consumers, including the well educated, easily justify using credit to pay for necessary expenses, especially after being convinced that 'no payments [for 12 months]' will provide enough time to come up with the money. With so much credit so readily available, it's no wonder that people get in over their heads."[8]

Interest rates and fees add to card users' troubles. For example, a household with the average amount of credit card debt in the survey ($8,650) would pay an additional $1,100 in costs each year if its card's interest rate was increased from the typical 12 percent to the average 25 percent "default rate" for one late payment.[9] Ultimately, the family is not able to keep up with the monthly payments and winds up in bankruptcy.

The credit card industry championed bankruptcy reform with the idea that the number of bankruptcy filings would decrease. But it is the credit card industry that perpetuates the debt-to-bankruptcy cycle. A September 2007 study by a University of Iowa professor found that nearly 100 percent of more than 300 families surveyed had been offered credit cards within a year of finishing up Chapter 7 bankruptcy. Nearly 88 percent of them reported that lenders had referenced the debtor's bankruptcy in the credit card solicitation. Thus, it appears that banks intentionally seek out recent bankruptcy filers as new customers.[10] Creditors know that other debts have been discharged and that it will be several years before the debtor can seek bankruptcy protection again. So the creditors, once again, take advantage of the debtor's desperate financial situation.

Debtors use "payday loans" and "easy credit" schemes as a short-term remedy.

Many studies have been conducted concerning the demographics of those who file for bankruptcy or seek consumer credit counseling services. The results generally indicate that these individuals fall into four general categories: ethnic minorities, women, the poor, and the elderly—groups that generally have

FTC Consumer Alert: Payday Loans = Costly Cash

Consumers should be very careful in using payday loans and in choosing a payday lender. The Federal Trade Commission (FTC) advises consumers to consider other alternatives before choosing a payday loan:

When you need credit, shop carefully. Compare offers. Look for one with the lowest annual percentage rate (APR)—consider a small loan from your credit union or small loan company, an advance on pay from your employer, or a loan from family or friends. A cash advance on a credit card also may be a possibility, but it will have a higher interest rate than your other sources of funds: Find out the terms before you decide. Also, a local community-based organization may make small business loans to individuals.

Compare the APR and the finance charge (which includes loan fees, interest, and other types of credit costs) of credit offers to get the lowest cost.

Ask your creditors for more time to pay your bills. Find out what they will charge for that service—as a late charge, an additional finance charge, or a higher interest rate.

Make a realistic budget, and figure your monthly and daily expenditures. Avoid unnecessary purchases—even small daily items. Their costs add up. Also, build some savings—even small deposits can help—to avoid borrowing for emergencies, unexpected expenses, or other items. For example, by putting the amount of the fee that you would pay on a typical $300 payday loan in a savings account for six months, you would have extra dollars available. This can give you a buffer against financial emergencies.

Find out if you have, or can get, overdraft protection on your checking account. If you are regularly using most or all of the funds in your account and if you make a mistake in your checking (or savings) account ledger or records, overdraft protection can help protect you from further credit problems. Find out the terms of overdraft protection.

If you need help working out a debt repayment plan with creditors or developing a budget, contact your local consumer credit counseling service. There are nonprofit groups in every state that offer credit guidance to consumers. These services are available at little or no cost. Also, check with your employer, credit union, or housing authority for no- or low-cost credit counseling programs.

If you decide you must use a payday loan, borrow only as much as you can afford to pay with your next paycheck and still have enough to make it to the next payday.

Source: Federal Trade Commission Consumer Alert. Available online at http://www.ftc.gov/bcp/conline/pubs/alerts/pdayalrt.shtm.

less education and lower incomes as a result of past discrimination. These same categories of people are also most likely to seek financial assistance through financing mechanisms that offer fast cash at subprime rates. They do not find themselves in these situations because they are spendthrifts or poor money managers. The earnings of these low income families are simply inadequate to take care of their basic needs.[11]

These "fast-cash" financing mechanisms generally offer short-term loans with very high fees and include schemes such as using the borrower's car title as collateral and loaning money against anticipated income tax refunds and payday loans.[12] A payday loan or paycheck advance is a small, short-term loan that is intended to cover a borrower's urgent expenses until his or her next payday.[13] The problem is that, in many instances, the borrower cannot repay the money when it becomes due. Instead, he or she pays an additional fee and rolls over the debt. This additional fee, or finance charge, covers the creditor's costs associated with lending the money. The finance charge, also known as interest, is usually stated in terms of an "annual percentage rate" (APR).

How does this happen? It is really quite simple: These so-called payday lenders target individuals who do not qualify for loans through traditional financial methods, and they offer them an opportunity to borrow money for a short period and repay it from their next paycheck—hence, the name "payday loans." The individuals are required to leave a post-dated check or an active checking account number as well as pay an upfront fee.

Consider the following hypothetical situation: Andrew and Denise fell victim to such a scheme after eight years of a marriage marked by health problems. Andrew was hospitalized several times due to complications from a previous injury, but the couple had very limited health coverage that resulted in accumulating unpaid medical bills. Although they had sought assistance through a local consumer credit counseling service, they had to file for bankruptcy under Chapter 13. Immediately after the

Payday loans

About one in five military service members took out a payday loan in 2004. According to the Center for Responsible Lending, someone who borrows $325 pays an average of $800 in charges.

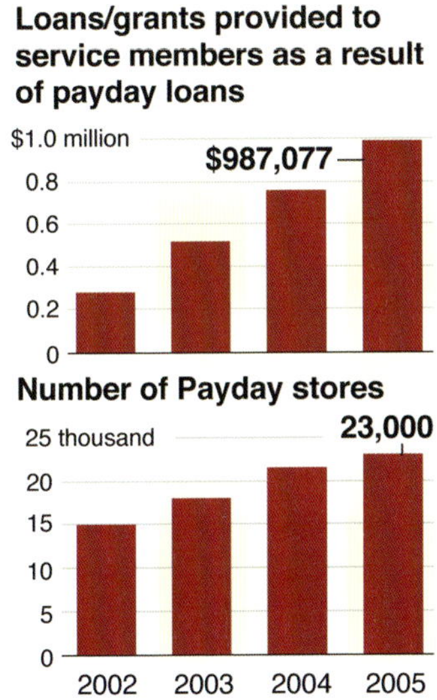

SOURCE: Department of Defense; Navy-Marine Corps Relief Society; Center for Responsible Lending — AP

A payday loan is a small, short-term loan that is intended to cover a borrower's urgent expenses until his or her next payday. These loans, however, often come at the price of high interest rates and collateral requirements.

bankruptcy, they felt some relief. Creditors had stopped calling and they had begun to pay their monthly obligations on time. They no longer dreaded answering their phone or going to the mailbox. They had managed to avoid foreclosure on their home, but there was no change in their income or in their spending needs.

When they needed $300 to pay their winter heating bill, Andrew borrowed it from a payday lender. The fee was $48 for a two-week loan that would be due on his next payday. Unfortunately, Andrew's car broke down on the way to work one day and he had to pay to get it repaired. That unforeseen cost meant that Andrew and Denise could not repay the $300 loan as planned. Instead, they paid an additional $48 to extend the payday loan for an additional two weeks. They extended the loan eight more times for various reasons, so that over a five-month period, they paid more than $400 in fees. This is an interest rate, or APR, of more than 400 percent, calculated over a year's time. And still, Andrew and Denise had not repaid the initial $300.[14]

A $48 fee for a $300 loan may seem worth it to someone who is strapped for cash and has no other source of funds. Payday lenders bank on this desperation. When the borrower is unable to repay the loan when it becomes due, he or she becomes dependent on the ability to extend the loan for a relatively small amount of money, and then continues to pay the extension fee over and over again. Even a modest fee of $10 on a loan of $100 payable in two weeks represents a 260 percent annual interest rate. Many times, what started out as a $100 loan very quickly turns into a debt of $1,000 or more. If the borrower cannot even pay the extension fee, the payday lender deposits the borrower's original post-dated check. If not enough funds are available in the borrower's bank account, he or she is charged a bank fee for insufficient funds and the payday lender is likely to charge a returned-check fee if the bank does not honor the check. In some instances, the payday lender will file criminal charges against the borrower for providing a "hot" check, even though the lender knew the borrower did not have the funds available to cover the check.

What is the alternative for these desperate borrowers? Without short-term cash flow assistance, they could find themselves not only bankrupt, but also homeless. Some proponents of payday loans see them as a godsend. Mary Jackson, of the payday lender trade group the Community Financial Services Association of America, says that "for someone with a phone bill due, no cash or credit, but a paycheck on the way, a single payday loan" provides a "valuable public and consumer service."[15] Payday loans are beneficial in other situations, as well:

> One common use of these fast payday loans is to cover any unexpected bills or financial expenses. In other words, would you take out a quick payday loan to cover all of your bills and pay only a one-time finance charge, or have your bank charge you a non-sufficient funds (NSF) charge of anywhere from $20 to $30 per bounced check? For instance, a $100 payday loan will cover any small checks such as a $50 phone bill or a $40 cable bill whereas your bank will charge you up to $30 per bounced item. To worsen matters, your bank may or may not cover those checks and if they do not, you will also incur a late charge from your phone or cable provider. If you took that route, then you could end up paying double for your phone or cable bill.
>
> Another advantage of getting these fast payday loans [is that they help] pay for unexpected situations such as car repairs. If you use your vehicle to commute to work and it suddenly breaks down on you, then what are you going to use to go to work, which helps pay for other daily necessities such as food, shelter, and clothing? With a quick payday loan, you can immediately get your car fixed and don't have to worry about receiving a smaller pay check.[16]

Proponents view payday loans as a viable option and even suggest that without payday loans, riskier borrowers such as bankruptcy filers would have no choices at all.

Banks and other traditional financial institutions should be the ones providing these short-term loans to consumers. Instead, it seems as though the banks have somehow collaborated with these lenders and created more ways of taking advantage of consumers. Banks charge comparably high rates through seemingly legitimate fees such as insufficient-funds charges, ATM fees, credit card late payment fees, and fees for overdraft protection services. Moreover, highly reputable banks such as Bank of America, JP Morgan Chase, Wells Fargo, U.S. Bancorp, and Wachovia fund payday lenders that are listed on major stock exchanges.[17] No matter which source a consumer chooses to take care of short-term cash needs, the banks come out ahead.

The real lesson here is quite clear: Borrower beware. If a payday loan or some other "easy credit" scheme seems to be the only alternative available, the consumer should at least shop around and obtain the best terms possible.[18]

Summary

There will probably be no change in the bankruptcy system until there is a change in the credit industry. Credit is easily available to consumers even if they are not credit-worthy or are a high credit risk. Those groups that are most vulnerable to these schemes are the same groups that are less likely to be able to pay their obligations as they become due—students, the underemployed or unemployed, elderly people, and those who are below the national poverty line.

Although most bankruptcies are the result of catastrophic life events, the crisis is usually aggravated by desperate financial decisions made by desperate consumers. Until the government and society address poverty relief and other social issues, consumers will continue to take desperate actions, live on credit cards, and take out payday loans. The cycle continues and these same consumers will find themselves in bankruptcy court again.

Bankruptcy Reform Continues

The number of bankruptcy filings continues to rise. There are many reasons why debtors take this route: They may have lost their jobs or experienced some other reduction in income. They may have incurred extraordinary medical expenses or experienced serious life events such as divorce or the death of a close family member. Sometimes debtors must file for bankruptcy because they have overextended on credit, are facing home foreclosure, or are simply victims of poor financial planning.

Regardless of the reason for filing, debtors look to the bankruptcy system to find financial relief. The bankruptcy discharge gives debtors the opportunity for a fresh start, and mandatory credit counseling from qualified institutions gives them the tools necessary for a meaningful financial recovery.

Bankruptcy Reform and Subprime Mortgages

Homeowners are now seeking help with their home mortgages as they struggle to make payments amid job losses and climbing interest rates on adjustable-rate mortgages. (An adjustable rate mortgage, or ARM, is a loan agreement in which the interest rates are adjusted periodically. As the interest rate rises, so does the monthly payment.) Under the current law, home mortgages are not protected in bankruptcy. In a 2007 blog about credit and bankruptcy, Professor Robert Lawless of the University of Illinois College of Law explained how a Chapter 13 bankruptcy currently affects home mortgages.[1] He explains that a Chapter 13 debtor must pay all secured claims in full, with interest. Any income that remains after paying for living expenses must go to payment of the unsecured claims for the next three or five years. If that remaining income were enough to pay the unsecured claims in full, the debtor typically would not be in bankruptcy. Therefore, unsecured claims are usually not paid in full through a Chapter 13 plan. Professor Lawless gives the following example:

> Suppose a secured creditor is owed $300,000 and has a claim against collateral with a value of $200,000. Under the general principles just outlined, a Chapter 13 plan would have to pay the secured creditor the full value of $200,000 including interest. The judge would determine the appropriate interest rate, which would be based on current market rates and not necessarily the rate in the loan agreement. The remaining $100,000 would be lumped with the other unsecured claims, and receive a proportional share, without interest, of the debtor's disposable income over the three- or five-year life of the Chapter 13 plan. These are general rules that apply to most unsecured claims.[2]

Lawless goes on to explain that home mortgages have always been an exception to these general rules and mortgage lenders

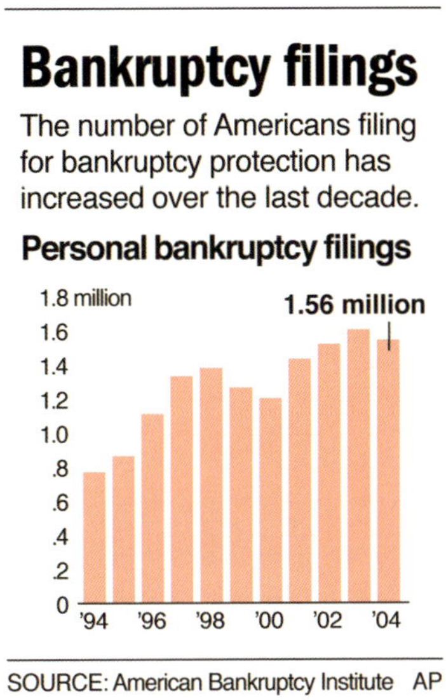

As the graph above shows, the number of Americans filing for bankruptcy rose from 1994 to 2004. As this trend continues, many people are calling out for reforms to the bankruptcy system.

have received special protection or preferential treatment that has not been given to other creditors:

> Thus, the U.S. Bankruptcy Code says that a Chapter 13 plan cannot modify secured claims on a debtor's principal residence. The U.S. Supreme Court has interpreted this provision to mean that a Chapter 13 plan must pay the full value of the secured creditor's claim, i.e., the full $300,000 in the example above. In bankruptcy talk, we say that a Chapter 13 debtor cannot "strip down" the mortgage to equal the value of the residence. The 2005 changes to the bankruptcy law extended the Chapter 13 anti-"strip down" rules to car loans made

> within two-and-a-half years of bankruptcy and all loans with one year of bankruptcy that fund the purchase of the asset serving as collateral for the loan (called a "purchase money security interest"). Also, bankruptcy judges cannot change the interest rates on home mortgages even if the current interest rate is much higher or lower than the interest rate at the time the loan was made. Thus, . . . loans on a principal residence get all sorts of special treatment.[3]

The only relief that might be available to the debtor is that the mortgage company might agree to be included as a part of a Chapter 13 repayment plan. Mortgage companies can voluntarily modify the terms of the mortgage loan to help borrowers, but they are not required to do so. Moreover, under current law, a bankruptcy judge cannot force a mortgage company to work with the debtor.

Legislation has been developed that might change this. Under a proposed bill known as the Miller-Sanchez Emergency Homeownership and Mortgage Equity Protection Act of 2007,[4] bankruptcy judges would be given the power to order loan modifications to help homeowners afford their mortgage payments. The bill would primarily affect homeowners who file Chapter 13 bankruptcy petitions with the intent to repay their debts over time. Judges would have broad discretion to order reductions in interest rates or extensions of time. The downside of this proposal is that mortgage lenders might be even more hesitant about providing mortgages to certain people.

Another problem is that this legislation applies only to homeowners with subprime and nontraditional loans, such as interest-only or optional payment loans, taken out since January 1, 2000, who file for bankruptcy relief, giving bankruptcy judges the power to manipulate subprime lending. Subprime lending—also known as B-paper, near-prime, or second chance lending—is the practice of making loans to borrowers who fail to qualify for the best market interest rates because of their deficient credit history. The term *subprime* refers to the credit status of the borrower being less than ideal, not the interest rate on the loan itself. In fact, a subprime loan is offered at a rate higher than other loans due to the increased risk.

Despite bipartisan opposition, the U.S. House Judiciary Committee recently passed a modification of the Miller-Sanchez bill. The modified bill, sponsored by House Judiciary Committee Chairman John Conyers Jr. (D-MI), would provide some relief to those homeowners who hold subprime and other nontraditional mortgages that they are now unable to pay. Under this bill, not only would bankruptcy judges be able to manipulate interest rates and excessive fees, but they would also be able to adjust the principal mortgage amount to reflect the current market value of the property. Under this proposed plan, both the borrower and the lender win. The borrower's payments would be lowered and there is a good chance that the creditor would be able to recover the loan.[4]

There is no question that the passage of this or a similar bill would cause an increase in the number of Chapter 13 bankruptcy filings. There could be a surge in filings similar to what occurred

Banks report record losses as a result of subprime lending market

During the US housing boom, the sub-prime market expanded significantly. These loans were provided to consumers with limited or poor credit histories. With the rise of interest rates and record unemployment, many sub-prime borrowers could no longer afford their monthly payments, causing them to default on loans." As a result, many banks were hit very badly. Some of the largest U. S. banks reported a drop in revenues of as much as 70 percent.

Source: Adapted from a story from BBC NEWS (published January 15, 2008). Available online at http://news.bbc.co.uk/2/hi/business/7188909.stm.

in 2005 with the initial passage of bankruptcy reform legislation. After all, this might be a debtor's only hope to avoid foreclosure when: (a) the debtor can no longer make the payments because of excessive ARMs; and (b) the amount owed on the mortgage far exceeds the market value of the home, so the debtor cannot pay off the loan, even if he or she were able to sell the house.

It is true that modifying the terms of a subprime mortgage would be beneficial. The homeowner is more likely to avoid foreclosure and keep his or her home. The mortgage company gets paid at least what it would get in foreclosure and does not have to write off the entire loan as a bad debt. But what about the investors who hold the debt?

There is another issue that should be considered, however, in addressing the subprime mortgage crisis. Nearly 75 percent of all subprime loans extended in 2004 and 2005 were bundled together and then sold in the secondary capital market. The owners of the loans are often foreign investors, and include groups such as pension plans, individual investors, insurance companies, and mutual fund companies. In other words, mortgage companies no longer own the subprime mortgage loans. They are merely engaged to run the operations. They have no power to negotiate with troubled debtors or to modify the terms of the loan—even if ordered by a court to do so. This arrangement makes it difficult to restructure these subprime mortgages. It will be very interesting to see how Congress resolves this dilemma.

Bankruptcy Reform and Student Loans

Student loans are one of the most difficult debts to avoid because they are not dischargeable in bankruptcy. Under the old law, student loans made by nonprofit organizations or governmental entities were dischargeable if the debtor could show undue hardship. Under the new law, a student loan cannot be discharged regardless of whether it was made by a nonprofit organization, a for-profit organization, a governmental entity, or a private commercial entity. In other words, no student loan can be discharged unless the debtor shows undue hardship. The obvious purpose of this prohibition is to protect governmental and private investments in education by preventing borrowers from abusing the system.

Bankruptcy courts generally look at three factors to determine undue hardship.[5] These factors are:

- Poverty: If the debtor were forced to repay the loan, he or she would be unable to maintain a minimal standard of living.
- Persistence of the hardship: There is evidence that this hardship will continue for a significant portion of the loan repayment period.
- Good faith: The debtor made good-faith efforts to repay the loan before filing for bankruptcy. (For example, the debtor has made payments for at least five years before seeking a discharge.)

The "undue hardship" standard is generally interpreted to mean that the debtor cannot maintain even a minimum standard of living if he or she has to repay the student loan. This is a very tough standard to meet, and bankruptcy filers often find themselves having to pay back these loans even when their other debts have been discharged in bankruptcy. Absent a showing of substantial hardship, the best that bankruptcy can do with respect to student loans may be to eliminate other debts that compete for the borrower's dollars.[6] There are, however, other options available to the borrower who is having trouble repaying his or her student loans. These options include, but are not limited to the following: deferment, in which scheduled student loan payments can be postponed for various reasons, such as unemployment, economic hardship, or enrollment as a student; or forbearance, in which payments are reduced or the repayment period is extended in order to prevent default.

Although there continues to be no relief from student loans made by governmental and nonprofit organizations, in June

2007, U.S. Senator Dick Durbin introduced legislation that would allow student loans from private financial institutions to be discharged after a debtor files for bankruptcy. He said:

> Private student loans are the fastest growing and most profitable sector of the student loan industry. Since 2001 the market for private student loans has grown at an annual rate of 27 percent to $17.3 billion in 2006—roughly 20 percent of total student borrowing. Ten years ago, only 5 percent of total education loan volume was in private loans. The interest rates and fees on private loans can be as onerous as credit cards. There are reports of private loans with interest rates of at least 15 percent and higher rates are not unheard of. Unlike federal student loans, there is no government-imposed loan limit on private loans and no public regulation over the terms and cost of these loans.[7]

Under the Durbin bill, private companies that provide student loans will be in the same position as virtually all other private lenders.

This proposed legislation has raised significant debate among bankruptcy judges and attorneys. Many argue that allowing discharges of student loans would lead to abuse of both the bankruptcy laws and the student loan program. The result would be an increase in the interest rates that lenders will impose. It could also mean that borrowers would no longer be able to access educational loans, thereby making it virtually impossible for many Americans to attend college or obtain other training.

Others believe that school loans should be discharged if a borrower files for bankruptcy. They contend that this may be the only way to deal with private trade schools that promise to provide marketable skills but fail to deliver on the promise. Perhaps the reason that student loans are not dischargeable is that an educated debtor is believed by some to be more financially able to take care of his or her debts than an uneducated debtor. After all, increased earning potential is one of the primary reasons that a person seeks education beyond secondary school.

But some private trade schools—such as business, computer, and cosmetology schools—go out of business before the borrower finishes the program. A prime example of the sham trade school problem involves Silver State Helicopters, a Nevada-based company that, without warning, shut its doors on Super Bowl Sunday 2008 and filed for bankruptcy protection. As reported by the San Diego *Union-Tribune*, Silver State's 2,500 students around the country were left in a lurch because they still had to repay the $70,000 they borrowed to pay their tuition, without the benefit of having received their certification.[8]

Not only do some schools go out of business, but in some cases, completed training turns out to be useless when it comes to increasing earning potential. Borrowers should not have to pay the penalty for this. Supporters of the Durbin bill also make a "public purpose" argument that in light of current economic conditions, the government should be interested in retraining U.S. workers. It should therefore make allowances for student loans and provide some relief to borrowers who are victims, through no fault of their own, of these private trade school shams.

This is an interesting debate that affects many families in the United States. Congress must weigh the desire to allow the borrower the opportunity for a fresh financial start against the desire to protect the student loan program. The future of education in the United States hangs in the balance.

Summary

The Bankruptcy Abuse Prevention and Consumer Protection Act of 2005 has made an important impact on the U.S. bankruptcy system. Debtors now must carefully consider other alternatives before filing their bankruptcy petitions. Bankruptcy attorneys are more accountable for the accuracy and completeness of the filings. Creditors are better protected than ever before. Nonetheless, with a steady decline in the job market and mortgage foreclosures on the rise, Congress must continue to make changes to the system. The economic stability of the American family depends on it.

APPENDIX

Beginning Legal Research

The goals of each book in the Point-Counterpoint series are not only to give the reader a basic introduction to a controversial issue affecting society, but also to encourage the reader to explore the issue more fully. This Appendix is meant to serve as a guide to the reader in researching the current state of the law as well as exploring some of the public policy arguments as to why existing laws should be changed or new laws are needed.

Although some sources of law can be found primarily in law libraries, legal research has become much faster and more accessible with the advent of the Internet. This Appendix discusses some of the best starting points for free access to laws and court decisions, but surfing the Web will uncover endless additional sources of information. Before you can research the law, however, you must have a basic understanding of the American legal system.

The most important source of law in the United States is the Constitution. Originally enacted in 1787, the Constitution outlines the structure of our federal government, as well as setting limits on the types of laws that the federal government and state governments can enact. Through the centuries, a number of amendments have added to or changed the Constitution, most notably the first 10 amendments, which collectively are known as the "Bill of Rights" and which guarantee important civil liberties.

Reading the plain text of the Constitution provides little information. For example, the Constitution prohibits "unreasonable searches and seizures" by the police. To understand concepts in the Constitution, it is necessary to look to the decisions of the U.S. Supreme Court, which has the ultimate authority in interpreting the meaning of the Constitution. For example, the U.S. Supreme Court's 2001 decision in *Kyllo v. United States* held that scanning the outside of a person's house using a heat sensor to determine whether the person is growing marijuana is an unreasonable search—if it is done without first getting a search warrant from a judge. Each state also has its own constitution and a supreme court that is the ultimate authority on its meaning.

Also important are the written laws, or "statutes," passed by the U.S. Congress and the individual state legislatures. As with constitutional provisions, the U.S. Supreme Court and the state supreme courts are the ultimate authorities in interpreting the meaning of federal and state laws, respectively. However, the U.S. Supreme Court might find that a state law violates the U.S. Constitution, and a state supreme court might find that a state law violates either the state or U.S. Constitution.

Not every controversy reaches either the U.S. Supreme Court or the state supreme courts, however. Therefore, the decisions of other courts are also important. Trial courts hear evidence from both sides and make a decision, while appeals courts review the decisions made by trial courts. Sometimes rulings from appeals courts are appealed further to the U.S. Supreme Court or the state supreme courts.

Lawyers and courts refer to statutes and court decisions through a formal system of citations. Use of these citations reveals which court made the decision or which legislature passed the statute, and allows one to quickly locate the statute or court case online or in a law library. For example, the Supreme Court case *Brown v. Board of Education* has the legal citation 347 U.S. 483 (1954). At a law library, this 1954 decision can be found on page 483 of volume 347 of the U.S. Reports, which are the official collection of the Supreme Court's decisions. On the following page, you will find sample of all the major kinds of legal citation.

Finding sources of legal information on the Internet is relatively simple thanks to "portal" sites such as findlaw.com and lexisone.com, which allow the user to access a variety of constitutions, statutes, court opinions, law review articles, news articles, and other useful sources of information. For example, findlaw.com offers access to all Supreme Court decisions since 1893. Other useful sources of information include gpo.gov, which contains a complete copy of the U.S. Code, and thomas.loc.gov, which offers access to bills pending before Congress, as well as recently passed laws. Of course, the Internet changes every second of every day, so it is best to do some independent searching.

Of course, many people still do their research at law libraries, some of which are open to the public. For example, some state governments and universities offer the public access to their law collections. Law librarians can be of great assistance, as even experienced attorneys need help with legal research from time to time.

APPENDIX

Common Citation Forms

Source of Law	Sample Citation	Notes
U.S. Supreme Court	*Employment Division v. Smith*, 485 U.S. 660 (1988)	The U.S. Reports is the official record of Supreme Court decisions. There is also an unofficial Supreme Court ("S. Ct.") reporter.
U.S. Court of Appeals	*United States v. Lambert,* 695 F.2d 536 (11th Cir.1983)	Appellate cases appear in the Federal Reporter, designated by "F." The 11th Circuit has jurisdiction in Alabama, Florida, and Georgia.
U.S. District Court	*Carillon Importers, Ltd. v. Frank Pesce Group, Inc.,* 913 F.Supp. 1559 (S.D.Fla.1996)	Federal trial-level decisions are reported in the Federal Supplement ("F. Supp."). Some states have multiple federal districts; this case originated in the Southern District of Florida.
U.S. Code	Thomas Jefferson Commemoration Commission Act, 36 U.S.C., §149 (2002)	Sometimes the popular names of legislation—names with which the public may be familiar—are included with the U.S. Code citation.
State Supreme Court	*Sterling v. Cupp*, 290 Ore. 611, 614, 625 P.2d 123, 126 (1981)	The Oregon Supreme Court decision is reported in both the state's reporter and the Pacific regional reporter.
State Statute	Pennsylvania Abortion Control Act of 1982, 18 Pa. Cons. Stat. 3203-3220 (1990)	States use many different citation formats for their statutes.

Cases and Statutes

United States Constitution, Article I, Section 8, Clause 4

Authorizes Congress to enact uniform laws on the subject of bankruptcies throughout the United States.

Bankruptcy Abuse Prevention and Consumer Protection Act of 2005, Public Law No. 109–8 (2005), 11 U.S.C. § 101 *et seq.*

Amended Title 11 of the United States Code and made sweeping changes to American bankruptcy laws, affecting both consumer and business bankruptcies. Commonly referred to as BAPCPA or the Bankruptcy Reform Act.

***Local Loan Co. v. Hunt*, 292 U.S. 234 (1934)**

U.S. Supreme Court decision ruling that bankruptcy law gives the debtor a new opportunity in life unhampered by the pressure of pre-existing debt.

***Federal Trade Commission v. AmeriDebt Inc., et al.* Civil Action No. PJM 03–3317**

The Federal Trade Commission brought charges against AmeriDebt, a consumer credit counseling agency, as well as its owner and affiliates, claiming that AmeriDebt deceived consumers by selling them debt management plans instead of focusing on educating debtors about personal financial management as advertised.

Fair Debt Collections Practices Act. 15 U.S.C. §§ 1692–1692p, as amended by Public Law 109–351, §§ 801–02, 120 Stat. 1966 (2006)

Requires that debt collectors treat debtors fairly and prohibits certain methods of debt collection.

Helping Families Save Their Homes in Bankruptcy Act of 2007, S. 2136. 110th Congress (2007)

A bill (not yet enacted into law) that amends federal bankruptcy law to permit a bankruptcy plan to: (1) modify a loan secured by the principal residence (home mortgage) of a Chapter 13 debtor with regular income; and (2) provide for payment of such a loan at a fixed annual percentage rate of interest, over a 30-year period.

Emergency Homeownership and Mortgage Equity Protection Act of 2007, H.R. 3609, 110th Congress (2007)

A bill (not yet enacted into law) that gives bankruptcy judges the power to order loan modifications to help homeowners afford their mortgage payments. (Companion bill to S. 2136.)

A bill to amend title 11, United States Code, with respect to exceptions to discharge in bankruptcy for certain qualified educational loans, S.1561, 110th Congress (2007)

A bill (not yet enacted into law) to make private student loans dischargeable in bankruptcy.

Terms and Concepts

adjustable-rate mortgage
automatic stay
bankruptcy
Bankruptcy Abuse Prevention and Consumer Protection Act (BAPCPA)
bankruptcy estate
bankruptcy petition
collateral
consumer credit counseling
creditor
debt
debt consolidation
debtor
discharge
exempt property
exemptions
exigent circumstances
Federal Rules of Bankruptcy Procedure
fresh start
involuntary petition
judgment proof
liquidation
means test
nonexempt property
payday loan
personal financial responsibility counseling
petition
pre-petition debts
projected disposable income
reaffirmation agreement
rehabilitation
repayment plan
secured debt
seized property
straight bankruptcy
subprime lending
tax lien

trustee
unsecured debt
voluntary petition
wage-earner bankruptcy

NOTES

Introduction: Bankruptcy Abuse Prevention and Consumer Protection Act of 2005

1 Nathan Hurst, "Personal bankruptcy filings soar," *Detroit News*, December 2, 2007, http://www.detnews.com/apps/pbcs.dll/article?AID=/20071226/BIZ01/712260394.
2 Ibid.
3 Federal Reserve Statistical Release, "Consumer Credit Outstanding," September 8, 2005, http://www.federalreserve.gov/releases/g19/current/default.htm.
4 Teresa A. Sullivan, Elizabeth Warren, and Jay Lawrence Westbrook, *The Fragile Middle Class: Americans in Debt* (New Haven, Conn.: Yale University Press, 2000), 16
5 "New bankruptcy law ignores underlying causes of debt," *Daily Record*, November 8, 2005, http://findarticles.com/p/articles/mi_qn4180/is_20051108/ai_n15836591.
6 Ibid., 11.
7 The American Bar Association, *Guide to Credit & Bankruptcy Terror* (New York: Random House References, 2006), 201.
8 "Bankruptcy reform gave creditors too much," *Washington Post*, August 21, 2006, http://www.washingtonpost.com/wp-dyn/content/article/2006/08/19/AR2006081900413.html.
9 American Bar Association, *Guide to Credit & Bankruptcy*, 200.
10 Michelle J. White, "Personal Bankruptcy Law: Abuse Prevention Versus Debtor Protection" (April 2007). *American Law & Economics Association Annual Meetings. American Law & Economics Association 17th Annual Meeting.* Working Paper 49. Available at http://law.bepress.com/alea/17th/art49.
11 Ibid., 13
12 The Bankruptcy Abuse Prevention and Consumer Protection Act of 2005 (S. 256) was passed by the Senate in March 2005 and was approved by a vote of 302–126 in the House of Representatives on April 14, 2005. President Bush signed S. 256 into law on April 20, 2005.
13 American Bankruptcy Institute, "Bankruptcy Filing Statistics," www.abiworld.org.
14 Michelle J. White, "Bankruptcy Reform and Credit Cards," July 2007, University of California, National Bureau of Economic Research, Working Paper No. 13265, 2.
15 292 U.S. 234, 244 (1934).
16 Legal Information Institute of Cornell University, "The Federal Rules of Bankruptcy Procedures," http://www.law.cornell.edu/rules/frbp.
17 U.S. Courts, http://www.uscourts.gov/adminoff.html.
18 American Bar Association, *Guide to Credit & Bankruptcy*, 247.
19 For a more detailed discussion of the differences between Chapter 7 and Chapter 13 bankruptcy, see the U.S. Department of Justice Web site at www.usdoj.gov/ust.
20 George Wallace, speaking for the Coalition for the Implementation of Bankruptcy Reform, on July 26, 2005, to the Subcommittee on Commercial and Administrative Law of the Committee on the Judiciary, U.S. House of Representatives, Oversight Hearing on the Implementation of the Bankruptcy Abuse Prevention and Consumer Protection Act of 2005.
21 *Federal Trade Commission v. AmeriDebt, Inc. et al.*, Civil Action No. PJM 03–3317.

Point: Recent Reforms Help Prevent Abuse of Bankruptcy Laws

1 The United States Constitution (Article 1, Section 8, Clause 4) authorizes Congress to enact "uniform Laws on the subject of Bankruptcies throughout the United States."
2 O. Max Gardner, "Forgive Us Our Debts . . ." http://www.bankruptcy victoriatexas.com/bankruptcy_and_the_bible.html.
3 Katherine M. Porter, "Bankrupt Profits: The Credit Card Industry's Business Model for Postbankruptcy Lending," September 2007, University of Iowa Legal Studies Research Paper No. 07–26.

Counterpoint: Recent Reforms Delay the Debtor's Fresh Start

1 Stephen Elias, *The New Bankruptcy: Will It Work for You?* (Berkeley, Calif.: Nolo, 2006), 2, 32.

NOTES

2 eMediaWire Press Release, "Attorney Fees on the Rise Due to New Bankruptcy Laws," July 25, 2006, http://www.emediawire.com/releases/2006/7/emw415614.htm.

3 "National Association of Consumer Bankruptcy Attorneys (NACBA) Bankruptcy Law Anniversary Survey," October 4, 2006, http://www.thehastingsgroup.com/NACBASurvey/summary.html.

4 eMediaWire Press Release, "Attorney Fees on the Rise Due to New Bankruptcy Laws," quoting Dean Holt, case coordinator at E-OnlineBankruptcy.com.

5 American Bar Association, letter to the Congressional Subcommittee on Commercial and Administrative Law, Committee on the Judiciary, concerning "The Second Anniversary of the Enactment of the Bankruptcy Abuse Prevention and Consumer Protection Act [P.L. 109–8]: Are Consumers Really Being Protected Under the Act?" May 1, 2007, http://www.abanet.org/poladv/letters/bankruptcy/2007may01_BAPCPAh_l.pdf.

6 NACBA Anniversary Survey.

7 11 U.S.C. § 707(b)(4)(C-D).

Point: Mandatory Credit Counseling Benefits Consumers and Lenders

1 The Financial Services Roundtable is a public policy group that promotes the interests of member companies in legislative, regulatory, and judicial forums; it represents 100 of the largest integrated financial services companies that provide banking, insurance, and investment products and services to American consumers. http://www.fsround.org/.

2 PR Newswire, "Statement: Study Shows 'Poor Money Management' Is Top Reason for Bankruptcy; Credit Counseling Is Key Factor in Success of Bankruptcy Reform to Date," October 17, 2006, http://www.prnewswire.com/cgi-bin/stories.pl?ACCT=109&STORY=/www/story/10-17-2006/0004453744&EDATE=.

3 "Profiteering in a Non-Profit Industry: Abusive Practices in Credit Counseling," Permanent Senate Subcommittee on Investigations, April 13, 2005, http://purl.access.gpo.gov/GPO/LPS62165 [pdf].

4 11 U.S.C. §11(c)(1)

5 *In re Salazar*, 339 B.R. 622 (Bankr. S.D. Tex. 2006) (Isgur, J.), citing H.R. Rep. 109–31(I), at 104, 2005.

6 See 11 U.S.C. § 109(h)(4).

7 *In re Cleaver*, 333 B.R. 430 (Bankr. S.D. Ohio 2005) (Walter, J.).

8 *In re Tulper*, 345 B.R. 322, 2006 WL 1651710 (Bankr. D.Col. May 22, 2006).

9 *In re Petit-Louis*, 338 B.R. 132 (Bankr. S.D. Fla. March 1, 2006).

Counterpoint: Consumer Credit Counseling Is Counterproductive and Subject to Fraud

1 *In re Raymond*, Slip Copy, 2006 WL 1047033 (Bankr. D. N.H. April 12, 2006).

2 *In re Westenberger*, Slip Copy, 2006 WL 1105008 (Bankr. D.D. Fla. April 25, 2006).

3 National Consumer Law Center and Consumer Federation of America, "Credit Counseling in Crisis: The Impact on Consumers of Funding Cuts, Higher Fees and Aggressive New Market Entrants," April 9, 2003, www.consumerfed.org/pdfs/credit_counseling_report.pdf [pdf].

4 Mark Furletti, "Consumer Credit Counseling: Credit Card Issuers' Perspectives," Discussion Paper (September 2003), 3–4. http://www.philadelphiafed.org/pcc/papers/2003/ConsumerCreditCounseling_092003.pdf [pdf].

5 "Credit Counseling in Crisis: The Impact on Consumers of Funding Cuts, Higher Fees and Aggressive New Market Entrants," Report by the Consumer Federation of America and the National Consumer Law Center (April 2003), 10. http://www.consumerfed.org/pdfs/credit_counseling_report.pdf [pdf].

6 Internal Revenue Service, "Credit Counseling Compliance Project Report," May 15, 2006, http://www.irs.gov/pub/irs-tege/cc_report.pdf.

7 *Federal Trade Commission v. AmeriDebt, Inc. et al.*, Civil Action No. PJM 03–3317.

8 Federal Trade Commission News Release, "AmeriDebt Founder Settles FTC Deception Charges," January 9, 2006, http://robbevans.com/pdf/debtworksftc010906.pdf [pdf].

NOTES

9 Federal Trade Commission News Release, "FTC Settles with AmeriDebt: Company to Shut Down," March 21, 2005.
10 Nathan Hurst, "Personal bankruptcy filings soar."
11 "Bankruptcy filings increase in 2007," *Sioux City Journal*, March 10, 2008, http://siouxcityjournal.com/articles/2008/01/28/news/iowa/1605bbca0b750368862573de00113960.txt.

Point: Bankruptcy Laws Allow People to Rebuild Their Finances Responsibly

1 Porter, Katherine M. and Thorne, Deborah, "The Failure of Bankruptcy's Fresh Start." *Cornell Law Review*, Vol. 92, 2006. Available at SSRN: http://ssrn.com/abstract=894453.
2 Ibid., 87.
3 David Goch, Washington Legislative Counsel, Commercial Law League of America, citing a study conducted by the National Foundation for Credit Counseling (NFCC).
4 15 U.S.C. sections 1692 and following.
5 The Hon. Edith Jones, Judge United States Court of Appeals for the Fifth Circuit and former member of the National Bankruptcy Commission, Statement Before the Joint Hearing of the Senate Judiciary Committee and the Subcommittee on Commercial and Administrative Law of the House Committee on the Judiciary (March 11, 1999), http://judiciary.house.gov/legacy/106–353.htm.

Counterpoint: Bankruptcy Reforms Do Not Solve the Real Problem for Millions of Americans

1 Porter and Thorne, 93
2 Ibid., 87–88.
3 Ibid., 85.
4 See Porter.
5 ABA, *Guide to Credit & Bankruptcy*, 201.
6 Ibid.
7 Jeffrey Freedman, "New bankruptcy law ignores underlying causes of debt."
8 Peter Agostino, "Forgive Us Our Debts: A Closer Look at the New Bankruptcy Law," *Notre Dame Business*, Winter 2006, www.nd.edu/~ndbizmag/winter2006/bankruptcy_print.shtml.
9 Demos and the Center for Responsible Lending, "The Plastic Safety Net: The Reality Behind Credit Card Debt in America," http://www.responsiblelending.org/pdfs/DEMOS-101205.pdf.
10 Porter, http://ssrn.com/abstract=1004276.
11 Tamara Draut, "Debt: The New Safety Net," *Around the Kitchen Table* (April 22, 2007). http://www.demos.org/aroundthekitchentable/article.cfm?id=04220703.
12 Jane Bryant Quinn, "Dragged Down by Debt: People with shaky credit are getting suckered by risky loans against their paychecks, homes—and even cars." *Newsweek*, May 2007, 49.
13 Wikipedia, "Payday loans," http://en.wikipedia.org/wiki/Payday_loans.
14 Annual Percentage Rate (APR) based on calculations using a Payday Loan Calculator provided at http://www.creditprovide.com/calculator/payday-loancalculator.html. The calculations are based on interest rates on short-term loans.
15 "A Call for Payday Lending Reform," interview with Mary Jackson, chairperson of the Federal Affairs Committee of the Community Financial Services Association of America, http://www.npr.org/templates/story/story.php?storyId=9875136.
16 "Instant Payday Loans: For better or worse?" Hot Payday, http://www.hotpayday.com/payday-loans-opinions2.html.
17 Ben Popkin, "Payday Lenders Funded by Bank of America, Chase, WellsFargo, U.S. Bancorp, Wachovia," *The Consumerist*, http://consumerist.com/consumer/loansharks/payday-lenders-funded-by-bank-of-america-chase-wellsfargo-us-bancorp-wachovia-270636.php. See also Rick Jurgens, "Utilities and Payday Lenders: Convenient Payments, Killer Loans. A Report by the National Consumer Law Center," June 2007, http://www.nclc.org/reports/content/payday_utility.pdf[.pdf].
18 Charlene Komar Storey, "Get Off the Treadmill," *Credit Union Management* 30, no. 3 (March 2007): 56–59.

Conclusion: Bankruptcy Reform Continues

1 Robert Lawless, "Mortgages in Bankruptcy 101," *Credit Slips: A Discussion on Credit and Bankruptcy*, November 20, 2007, http://www.creditslips.org/creditslips/2007/11/mortgages-in-ba.html.

2 Ibid.

3 Ibid.

4 H.R. 3609, 110th Congress (2007).

5 "House Committee Votes on Mortgage Bankruptcy Bill," Mortgage News Daily (December 13, 2007). http://www.mortgagenewsdaily.com/12132007_Bankruptcy_Code_asp.

6 *Brunner v. New York State Higher Education Services Corp.*, 831 F.2d 295 (1987) at p. 1.

7 "Bankruptcy in Brief: A Service of the Moran Group." http://www.moranlaw.net/index.htm.

8 Mobilize.org, "Senator Introduces Bill with Student Loan Bankruptcy Provision," June 7, 2007, http://www.mobilize.org/index.php?tray=content&tid=top401&cid=272.

9 Bruce V. Bigelow, "Left in the Lurch," *San Diego Union-Tribune* (March 9, 2008). http://www.signonsandiego.com/uniontrib/20080309/news_lz1b9lenders.html.

RESOURCES

Books and Reports

American Bankruptcy Institute. "Bankruptcy Filing Statistics." Available online. URL: www.abiworld.org. Accessed March 14, 2008.

American Bar Association. *The American Bar Association Guide to Credit and Bankruptcy*. New York: Random House, 2006.

Elias, Stephen. *The New Bankruptcy: Will It Work For You?* Berkeley, Calif.: Nolo, 2005.

Epstein, David and Jonathan Landers. *Debtors and Creditors: Cases and Materials*. 2nd ed. Eagan, Minn.: West Publishing Company, 1982.

Internal Revenue Service. "Credit Counseling Compliance Project Report." IRS, May 15, 2006. Available online. URL: www.irs.gov/pub/irs-tege/cc_report.pdf. Accessed March 14, 2008.

Love, Tiffany R. *Surviving Financial Disasters*. Centreville, Va.: Petra Publishing, 2004.

Michael, Jeff and Thom Fox. *Repair Your Credit and Knock Out Your Debt*. New York: McGraw Hill, 2004.

Web Sites

U.S. Department of Justice: U.S. Trustee

http://www.usdoj.gov/ust/eo/bapcpa/index.htm

This site lists approved consumer credit counseling services, and has resources on how to report violations and fraud.

BAPCPA Blog

http://bapcpa.blogspot.com

The American Bankruptcy Institute blogs about important current events and issues.

American Bankruptcy Institute

http://www.abiworld.org

The American Bankruptcy Institute answers frequently asked questions and provides a list of publications on current bankruptcy issues.

Morgan King's Bankruptcy Media.com

http://bankruptcymedia.com

This Web site is a good source for case law and general articles on bankruptcy issues.

U.S. Bankruptcy Courts

http://www.uscourts.gov/bnkrpctystats/statistics.htm

The U.S. Bankruptcy Courts Web site provides bankruptcy statistics, the basics of bankruptcy law, links to other courts across the country, and an explanation of the Federal Rules of Bankruptcy Procedures.

Cornell University, Legal Information Institute

http://www.law.cornell.edu/topics/bankruptcy

Cornell University presents general information on bankruptcy as well as a discussion of certain court cases.

Federal Trade Commission

http://www.ftc.gov

General information about bankruptcy laws can be found on the FTC Web site, in addition to information about how to file complaints against credit reporting agencies, and Truth in Lending Act complaints.

National Foundation for Credit Counseling (NFCC)

http://www.nfcc.org/bankruptcy

Learn more about consumer credit counseling accreditation from this watchdog organization.

PICTURE CREDITS

PAGE

19: AP Images/R. Morris, C. Kaeser
30: AP Images/Jane Bell
69: AP Images/MS/JJO
75: AP Images/RM

INDEX

INDEX

SANDRA COAXUM ALLEN is an attorney and executive manager who lives in Canton, Michigan. She earned a BBA in Accounting from the University of Texas at Austin and a J.D. from the University of Texas School of Law. She has received certification as a public accountant and mediator. Ms. Allen is a director of procurement at the Wayne County Airport Authority. Licensed to practice law in the state of Texas for 20 years and a certified public accountant (CPA) for over 16 years, Mrs. Allen has held several executive management positions in the public and private sectors. She was an assistant attorney general at the Office of the Texas Attorney General and Chief of the Attorney General's Open Records Division. Upon leaving the public sector, Mrs. Allen became the Vice President of Business Development for a regional logistics and supply chain management firm based in Dallas, Texas. She then returned to the public sector to serve as executive director of a nonprofit organization that promotes literacy among elementary school students, where she worked until moving to Michigan.

ALAN MARZILLI, M.A., J.D., lives in Alabama, and is a program associate with Advocates for Human Potential, Inc., a research and consulting firm based in Sudbury, Massachusetts, and Albany, New York. He primarily works on developing training and educational materials for agencies of the federal government on topics such as housing, mental health policy, employment, and transportation. He has spoken on mental health issues in 30 states, the District of Columbia, and Puerto Rico; his work has included training mental health administrators, nonprofit management and staff, and people with mental illnesses and their families on a wide variety of topics, including effective advocacy, community-based mental health services, and housing. He has written several handbooks and training curricula that are used nationally and as far away as the territory of Guam. He managed statewide and national mental health advocacy programs and worked for several public interest lobbying organizations while studying law at Georgetown University. He has written more than a dozen books, including numerous titles in the POINT/COUNTERPOINT series.